KIDNAPPED IN ROME

PETER REESE DOYLE

PUBLISHING

Colorado Springs, Colorado

KIDNAPPED IN ROME

Copyright © 1996 by Peter Reese Doyle
All rights reserved. International copyright secured.

Library of Congress Cataloging-in-Publication Data
Doyle, Peter Reese.
Kidnapped in Rome / Peter Reese Doyle
     p. cm. — (A Daring adventure ; 9)
  Summary: While sightseeing in Rome, siblings Penny and Mark and their friend David
find themselves mixed up with a group of political terrorists and kidnappers who are using
counterfeit money to try to frame prominent bankers and government officials.
    ISBN 1-56179-480-5
  [1. Adventure and adventurers—Fiction. 2. Brothers and sisters—Fiction.
3. Rome (Italy)—Fiction. 4. Christian life—Fiction.] I. Title.
II. Series: Doyle, Peter Reese, 1930– Daring Family adventures ; bk. 9.
PZ7.D777Ki 1996
  [Fic]—dc20   96-5781
                                                           CIP
                                                           AC

Published by Focus on the Family Publishing,
Colorado Springs, Colorado 80995

Distributed in the U.S.A. and Canada by Word Books, Dallas, Texas.

This is a work of fiction, and any resemblance between the characters in this
book and real persons is coincidental.

Focus on the Family books are available at special quantity discounts when purchased
in bulk by corporations, organizations, churches, or groups. Special imprints, messages,
and excerpts can be produced to meet your needs. For more information, write:
Special Sales, Focus on the Family Publishing, 8605 Explorer Drive, Colorado Springs,
CO 80920, or call (719) 531-3400 and ask for the Special Sales Department.

Cover Design: AvreaFoster
Cover Illustration: Benjamin Vincent

Printed in the United States of America

96 97 98 99 00/10 9 8 7 6 5 4 3 2 1

CONTENTS

CHAPTER 1

THE RUINS OF ANCIENT ROME

The three Americans split off from the group of tourists who had just followed their guide into the interior of the ancient Roman Colosseum. While the others moved on, Mark and Penny Daring and their friend David Curtis shaded their eyes with their hands and gazed up at the steeply slanted tiers of seats.

The massive brown stone structure towered high above them, making the three feel small and insignificant. Exposure to 20 centuries of weather had worn the stones of the giant building; they were cracked, rounded, crumbled. Yet visitors who stood within the historic Colosseum were overwhelmed by its vast dimensions and by the rows and rows of seats that loomed above them.

The massive structure that had dominated the city of Rome for almost two thousand years held the three young Americans speechless for a moment, then Mark broke the silence.

"Wow!" he exclaimed. "When was this built?"

Mark Daring was a strongly built young man of 17, with

blue eyes and blond hair. He wore white slacks and a dark-blue polo shirt. He shaded his eyes with his hands as he gazed at the highest remaining wall of the stadium.

David, also 17, was scanning the pages of his guidebook. David was six feet one, taller than Mark by two inches, and slender, yet every bit as strong. His hair was dark, his eyes brown, and he had a lean face and perpetually cheerful expression. David wore dark trousers and a maroon shirt. He looked up from his book and answered Mark's question.

"When was this built? The Emperor Vespasian began the work in 72 A.D., but it was his son, Titus, who opened it for contests eight years later. They made a big deal of the opening games and held them for a hundred days, in fact."

Still gazing up at the top of the Colosseum wall, Mark asked, "What kind of games?"

"Athletic contests of all kinds," his sister replied. "I read about this before. But they also fought wild animals here. Over the centuries, they killed thousands and thousands of lions, elephants, zebras—all kinds of animals." She shuddered at the thought.

A year younger than the two boys, Penny was slender, with light-brown hair, and the prettiest brown eyes David Curtis had ever seen. For lunch that day, the three were going to meet Mr. Daring and his Italian friend, Antony Bellini, at a nice restaurant in the city, so Penny was wearing a sleeveless white dress with white shoes.

"It was a bloodthirsty age, all right," Mark said, thinking of all the killing that had occurred on this site.

"Well," David said, his brown eyes thoughtful, "the

Romans couldn't have seen as much bloodshed in a lifetime as most of the people in America see each year on television. You two have been in Africa for some years, and you wouldn't believe the things families watch back home."

David Curtis lived in Montgomery, Alabama, and had spent the summer with the Darings in their home in East Africa, where the headquarters of Mr. Daring's mining engineering company was located. Both Mr. Daring and Mr. Curtis were mining engineers, in fact, and the two families had known each other for years.

Penny looked across the cavernous building and scanned the weathered stone seats on the other side. The sun was bright this July day, and she shaded her eyes with her hand.

"I wonder how many people could fit into this huge place?" she asked David. She turned and smiled up at him as the three began to saunter around the walkway at the bottom row of seats.

"The book says it held 55,000," David replied, tearing his eyes away from hers with some difficulty. He pointed and said, "And see over there? They built side halls around the inside of the place so that the whole crowd could get in and out in a hurry. They could fill the place in 10 minutes."

David stumbled on a rough stone, then recovered his balance as he told more about the activities that had taken place within the ancient Colosseum. "The Romans made lots of circus animals do tricks. They brought animal trainers and their animals from all over the Empire. And after the circus tricks, they'd let animals fight each other. And like you said, Penny, they'd send men to fight the wild animals."

"And what's worse, didn't they also make men fight each other to death?" Penny asked.

"They sure did," David answered. "Sometimes slaves fought each other, and sometimes they used soldiers the Romans had captured in their wars."

Mark stopped and pointed down at the remaining walls of rooms in the exposed floor of the stadium. Below the floor there had been several levels with chambers and cages, where animals of all kinds had been kept. There were also rooms for their keepers and trainers, as well as for supplies and food.

Mark looked around the building again, his normally pleasant face sobered by his thoughts. "So this is where so many Christians were killed by wild animals for the amuse-ment of the Roman crowds."

"That's right," David said.

"But it must have cost a fortune to bring all those animals and men from all over the world, and keep and feed them here!" Penny remarked. "Who paid for all that?"

"The emperors and wealthy citizens," David explained. "It was a kind of welfare system. As the Roman Empire expanded, the government bureaucracy did, too. They began to issue hundreds of regulations for the people and for their busi-nesses. This finally messed up the Roman economy, caused it to stagnate, in fact, and many thousands of people were thrown out of work."

"We studied that in history," Penny reminded her brother. "Remember all the parallels between the Roman Empire and the United States today?"

"Yes, I sure do," Mark replied. "And they're scary."

"They really are," David agreed. "Anyway, with so many thousands of able-bodied men out of work, the city began to have terrible problems with crime. So the government and wealthy aristocrats paid these people *not* to work and then paid for the games and fights in the Colosseum to keep them happy. It kept the populace from rioting."

At the beginning of the summer, David had flown from the United States to visit Mark and Penny Daring, and since then, the three had had some remarkable adventures. Mr. Daring's business had taken him to Egypt, France, Greece, Germany, and now Italy. His firm was raising investment capital for two major projects in East Africa and Egypt, and he'd taken the three teenagers with him on his trips. He said he needed them to handle some of his computer work and communications, and they had been quite useful to him. But he and Mrs. Daring had also wanted the youngsters to have the experience of traveling in Europe.

What Mr. and Mrs. Daring had not planned on were the troubles that had followed the three teenagers wherever they'd gone. In Africa, they had first encountered Hoffmann, formerly of the East German Secret Police. This man had almost captured them in Egypt and again in France. He'd stalked them in Germany, too. But now the Americans were sure that they were free of all such dangers and were looking forward to their brief visit to Italy.

Mrs. Daring had visited them for a couple of days after their adventures in Germany and had just flown back to her smaller children in East Africa that morning. Mark, Penny, and David were spending a couple of hours touring the ancient ruins of Rome while Mr. Daring met with his Italian banker, Mr. Bellini.

The three teenagers were fascinated by history. Penny was also a serious photographer, and today, as on all their trips, she stopped the boys periodically so she could study a scene and find the best angle for her photographs. She stopped them now as she removed the wide-angle lens from the camera case slung over her shoulder and put it in place of the telephoto lens, which she put back into the case. Then she framed a careful picture.

"Thanks," she said to Mark and David as she closed up her camera. "I can't get over how much history is here!"

They strolled out of the Colosseum and away from the structure so Penny could take more pictures of it from outside. Then they turned and looked back at the massive pile of stone.

"Look at the differences in those columns," Penny said, pointing.

"They just look like columns to me," her brother said, pretending to yawn. "You probably think you see something, though. What is it?"

"I'm not sure I should waste such insights on the ignorant," she said with a straight face, "but they *are* different columns on the different levels. They've got different decorations on the tops of them. You've got to learn to notice such things, Mark!"

The boys were always amazed at the things Penny noticed —things they often neglected to see. Penny's mom was a serious photographer herself and had taught Penny to be keenly observant. This skill had served the three teenagers well in several of their adventures earlier in the summer.

Walking farther away from the majestic Colosseum, they passed other old stone buildings, marveling that so many of the ancient works had survived to the end of the twentieth century. Finally, they came to one of the most famous of the historic sights, the massive Arch of Titus, which had stood in place since 81 A.D. Penny stopped again and took pictures. On the stone Arch were carved representations of the treasures the Roman armies had taken from the city of Jerusalem when they captured it in 70 A.D.

"Look at that!" she exclaimed excitedly. "I got pictures of the altar, the silver trumpets, and the seven-branched golden candlestick they took from the Jerusalem temple! Imagine being able to see all this!"

The three had read of the terrible siege of Jerusalem by the Roman armies under Titus and of the destruction of the city and the massacre of its people. After the city's destruction, the surviving Jews had been scattered around the Roman Empire.

"What caused the Romans to attack and destroy Jerusalem?" Mark asked.

"A Jewish group called the 'Zealots' killed a Roman garrison and called for a holy war," David replied. "They claimed that God had told them to rise up against Roman rule."

"Didn't the Jewish leaders tell the people that those rebels were false prophets?" Mark asked.

"You bet they did!" David said, his face animated. "But the Zealots always found enough people to follow when they

called for terrorism and claimed they were fighting for jus-
tice. The same thing has happened many times in history. It's
happened in this century, in fact."

Just then, Mark glanced at his watch. "Hey!" he exclaimed,
blue eyes sparkling, his broad face breaking into a smile. "I
hate to interrupt our walk through history, but look what time
it is. We've got to get back and meet Dad for lunch."

Penny threw a pitying glance at her brother. "Oh, Mark,
can't you think of anything but food? I haven't nearly finished
taking pictures."

"I'm *not* thinking of food, Penny," Mark protested. "Dad's
expecting to meet us in 20 minutes. We've got to hurry if we
don't want to keep him waiting. As for food, you know me—
I can take it or leave it. It's Dad I'm thinking about."

"Oh, you're so noble, Mark," she replied with a laugh.
"But of course you're right. We can't keep Dad waiting." She
packed up her camera and smiled at David. He grinned back,
and the three turned and walked toward the restaurant.

CHAPTER 2

THE MESSENGER

The three teenagers arrived at the restaurant to find Mr. Daring and his friend waiting for them. Jim Daring introduced them to Mr. Antony Bellini, the banker he'd come to Rome to see. Bellini was tall, with broad shoulders, graying black hair, and a magnificent mustache on his long, distinguished-looking face. Mark and David were impressed with the man's powerful build. Bellini's dark eyes beamed with good humor as he greeted Mark, Penny, and David.

"Welcome to Rome!" he said in a deep voice, as he shook their hands. "I hope you have had a pleasant visit so far."

His English was excellent, but flavored with an accent.

The three assured him that they were enjoying themselves, and the group moved into the restaurant. Mr. Bellini waved for the head waiter, who had reserved a table for him and his guests.

They were seated, and Mr. Bellini helped the Americans to order. Then the Italian banker asked the teenagers to tell him what they had seen of the city so far. They described those parts of the Forum that they'd explored, and Penny told of the pictures she had taken.

"Excellent, excellent!" he commented, smiling. "But you must see the area called the Palatine! It is a very relaxing place—a huge park, with ruins of ancient temples and palaces of the emperors. The great Augustus himself had a modest home there. He was emperor when Christ was born, you remember."

During the meal, their charming host told them of the city's many tourist sites.

"I regret that you have so few days to see this city!" he said, dark eyes shining.

Jim Daring laughed. "Antony, I told you I've got to work for a living. I can't quit my job just so these three can wander around Rome for the summer."

"A pity, a pity," Antony Bellini replied. "In any case, my wife and I are so pleased that you are coming to stay with us tonight in our country villa. Actually, Jim, you and Mrs. Daring and these three should have come to our home when you first arrived in Rome."

"Antony, you're too kind," Mr. Daring said. "We didn't want to inconvenience you for so long, so we thought we should stay in a hotel at first. But we're delighted to come to your home this afternoon. Thanks again for the invitation."

"You are most welcome, all of you! My wife, Teresa, is delighted to have you visit with us." Then he looked at the teenagers and said, "After lunch, perhaps you young people would like to explore the famous Palatine while Jim and I complete our business. Then we can all meet later and go out to my home in the country."

As they were finishing the last of their meal and making

arrangements for the afternoon, a smooth voice suddenly broke in. "Pardon, Señor Bellini."

They all looked up to see a pale young man in a dark suit appear at Mr. Bellini's side. The man handed Mr. Bellini a letter.

"Ah, Alberto!" Mr. Bellini said with a smile, as he took the letter. "This must be urgent if they sent you to find me at lunch. Let's speak English, please, and I'll introduce you to my American friends."

Alberto flashed a quick smile as he acknowledged the introductions. Then his face grew solemn. "Yes, Mr. Bellini, Mr. Rossini told me it was urgent." Something fell from Alberto's hand suddenly, and the young man stooped to retrieve it.

"Sorry," he said as he stood. "I dropped my pen."

He held up his pen nonchalantly. But none of them had seen the man place a small black object on the floor, nor did anyone see him slide this under the table with the toe of his shoe. Alberto straightened and began to gaze intently at Mr. Bellini while the banker looked at the envelope. He seemed to have forgotten the Americans completely.

Penny watched Alberto as he riveted his attention on the banker. *He's studying Mr. Bellini's reaction to the letter!* Penny thought. *I wonder what it says?*

"Pardon me, please," Mr. Bellini said to his guests with an apologetic smile. He hurriedly opened the letter and scanned its contents.

Penny glanced again at Alberto, and the young man's eyes were fixed on Mr. Bellini's. Then Penny saw a slight smile flash across Alberto's face. It vanished at once, to be replaced by a blank expression. She couldn't help but wonder if Alberto was up to something.

Mr. Bellini, meanwhile, studied the letter with intense concentration. A dark frown gathered on his large, expressive face. Then he looked up at Alberto. "Do you know the contents of this letter, Alberto?"

Alberto seemed surprised, Penny thought.

"No, sir. Mr. Rossini just handed it to me and told me to bring it to you right away."

His eyes wandered over to Penny, and he suddenly smiled. *It's almost as if he knew he'd been staring too hard at Mr. Bellini,* Penny thought. She looked down, afraid that her suspicion might show in her eyes, for she had a sudden sense that Alberto was not telling the truth. *I bet he* does *know what's in that letter,* she thought. *Something about the way he looked at Mr. Bellini didn't seem quite right.*

Mr. Bellini looked at the letter again. He sighed, then spoke to the messenger. "Thank you, Alberto. You can return to the bank."

Alberto seemed to hesitate. Penny guessed that he'd hoped to be let in on a discussion of the letter's contents. But the young man recovered quickly, forced a smile, and said, "Certainly, Mr. Bellini." He bowed politely to the others and left the restaurant, walking away rapidly.

Penny glanced at her dad and saw that he had been looking at her, as if he'd noticed her suspicion of Alberto. Mr. Daring raised an eyebrow, nodded slightly toward the retreating Alberto, then shot her a questioning expression. She frowned a little in return. Then they both looked over at their host.

A serious expression had settled upon Mr. Bellini's face. When he spoke, his voice was low and grave. "My friends, this letter is a warning from Mr. Rossini, our bank's executive vice president. He tells me to be on guard. We've discovered a spy in our organization, and we have reason to believe that someone is trying to trouble our bank. We have recently received deliveries of money that we discovered to be counterfeit."

The banker kept his voice low as he continued. "We believe that this is politically motivated. The police believe this also." Bellini looked over at Mr. Daring. "As you know, Jim, the chairman of the board of our bank is highly placed in Italy's government. He is a firm supporter of our present prime minister, whose policies have been unpopular with the socialists and others to the left. I also have been particularly outspoken in the business community in defending his policies. This letter Alberto brought me from Mr. Rossini is a warning that we may expect trouble because of our opposition to socialist and communist forces."

"What kind of trouble, Antony?" Jim Daring asked quickly. He leaned forward toward his friend.

"We're not sure, Jim. Mr. Rossini's letter, however, is a reminder that we must remain cautious." He folded the letter and replaced it in the envelope. Putting this in his coat pocket, he sighed and leaned back in his chair. "It's always possible, of course, that some of the bank's officers could be kidnapped."

This shocked the Americans.

"Are you in danger, Antony?" Jim Daring asked, a frown of concentration on his face.

"No, no, Jim," Bellini replied with a laugh. "But our president, perhaps, and the chairman of the board—they may be in danger of being kidnapped."

"Would that really happen, Mr. Bellini?" Mark asked.

"It certainly could, Mark," Bellini answered. "Socialists, remember, are totalitarians—in whatever country they live and scheme. They believe that they and they alone have the right and the brains to rule their nation. And they will let no one stand in their way, as the whole history of the twentieth century testifies!"

"Is there anything we can do to help you, Antony?" Jim Daring asked quietly.

"Thank you, Jim," the banker replied. "I do not know. But I appreciate your offer. Now I think that you and I should return to the bank to complete our business. And I must see Mr. Rossini briefly. He's the vice president of our bank, as I told you." He glanced over at the three teenagers. "You three go on to the Palatine, as I suggested. You won't be disappointed, I assure you."

"I'm sure they'll love it," Jim Daring said. "Can you show them how to get there, Antony?"

"Certainly."

David handed over the guidebook, and the banker unfolded the map in the back. He found the Palatine and leaned forward, pointing to where the teenagers would want to go. Handing back the guidebook, Mr. Bellini called for the check and paid for their lunch. "At 4:30, then," he said with a smile.

He rose from the table and led them from the room. The Americans thanked their host for the meal.

Suddenly, Jim Daring stopped. "Penny," he said, "I just remembered. I brought your raincoat with me and put it with mine in the checkroom. We can get them as we leave."

"Thanks, Daddy," she said. "Did you bring my guidebook, too?"

"Yes. I put it in the pocket of the coat. Are you sure you want to carry that coat around?"

"Oh, yes," she replied. "It's lightweight, and the rain can come suddenly here, they say."

They went to the checkroom, retrieved the coats, and stepped out of the restaurant and into the bright sunlight. Mr. Bellini asked the doorman to call a taxi. One came at once, and he and Jim Daring got in, waving good-bye to the teenagers as the cab drove off toward the bank.

"Now for the Palatine," David said with anticipation. "I've been wanting to tell you two about that area."

"Just keep the lectures brief," Mark advised. "After all, we've just eaten. My brain can only take in so much information after lunch."

Penny laughed at him. "Mark, your brain's probably as stuffed as your stomach. But don't worry, David, *I'm* still alert. Lecture on." She folded her coat over her arm and slung her camera case over her shoulder as the three walked toward the Palatine.

CHAPTER 3

THE COUNTERFEITERS

Alberto did not return to the bank when he left Mr. Bellini and the others. Instead, he directed his taxi to an office building a half mile away from the restaurant where he'd delivered the letter to Mr. Bellini.

Paying the cab driver, the young man rushed into the building and took the elevator up. A few moments later, he entered an office and was escorted by the secretary into a large room lined with tall bookcases filled with leather-bound books.

"Mr. Carlucci is expecting you," the secretary said to the young man.

The massive man behind the elaborate leather-covered desk did not smile when Alberto entered. He merely stared at the young man who came to a stop before him. Alberto fidgeted nervously and dropped his eyes before the big man's steely glare. Bushy eyebrows accentuated the force of Carlucci's steady gaze. A long white scar curved across his broad forehead. Powerful shoulders filled his expensive dark coat.

"There's been a mistake," Carlucci said finally. He sighed and lit a cigarette.

Shocked, Alberto started. *What did I do wrong?* he thought.

I did exactly what they told me to do! Beads of sweat began to form on his forehead.

As if he'd read the messenger's mind, Carlucci spoke again. "It was not your fault. Thomaso committed the error. But it may cause us trouble. It's *got* to be corrected at once!" He continued to stare at Alberto.

"What happened, sir?" the young man asked nervously, licking his lips and shifting on his feet. His heart was beating rapidly now.

"Were your men able to plant that package of counterfeit money on those Americans while they were eating with Bellini?"

"Yes, sir," Alberto replied. "Luis did that while I took the letter to Mr. Bellini. The girl and her father had put their raincoats in the checkroom of the restaurant before the meal, so Luis bribed the attendant and placed the money in the pocket of the girl's coat."

The big man gritted his teeth and muttered angrily to himself. Then he got control of his anger.

"You and Luis did exactly as you had been told, Alberto. But orders have been changed. It was decided *not* to implicate Mr. Bellini's friends as originally planned, but to kidnap Bellini instead. So we *must* get back those counterfeit bills! Who knows when that girl might discover them in her coat and what she might do with them. We must get them back immediately!"

"But, sir!" Alberto said. "What caused them to change the plan? We were supposed to plant those false bills on the Americans—which we did—then lead the police to arrest them. You were going to implicate Mr. Bellini through his American friends!"

"Yes, yes, I know what the plan *was*. But as for the change, that's not for you to ask, Alberto," Carlucci said sharply, his face darkening with anger. "You just do what I tell you. They now plan to kidnap Bellini himself and leave his friends out of this. They want to plant those bills instead in the office of the prime minister. The serial numbers on the bills are recorded, and these numbers have already been given to the Treasury officials. We've *got* to get back that package of money! Our whole plot may be exposed if we don't!"

"What do you want me to do, sir?" Alberto asked, a quaver in his voice.

"Retrieve that counterfeit money. Do you know where those American teenagers are right now?" Carlucci asked, viciously stubbing out his cigarette in the large ashtray on the desk. *This whole scheme is about to unravel!* he thought, fighting back a feeling of panic.

"Yes, sir, I do," Alberto stammered. His hands were trembling with fright. "They're planning to tour the Palatine until 4:30, sir. Then they'll meet Mr. Bellini and Mr. Daring. When I delivered the letter to Mr. Bellini, I placed a small mike under their table, and Luis was able to pick up their conversation after I had left. That's how we know their plans."

"Very good, Alberto!" Carlucci said grudgingly. He tapped his long forefinger on the desk as he thought. Then he smiled. "The Palatine? Well, well, well. With trees all around, that's the perfect place for Luis and his men to track those young Americans, take that girl's coat, and get back the bills!"

"There are two young men with that girl, sir," Alberto reminded him. "They look strong."

"Two teenagers against Luis and his men?" Carlucci asked, raising his eyebrow. "They had better stay out of the way or they'll get hurt. Now, listen! I want you to call Luis right away! Tell him to retrieve those counterfeit bills and bring them to me at once. You, meanwhile, will return to your bank as soon as you talk with Luis—before Mr. Rossini becomes suspicious and before Mr. Bellini returns and wonders where you've been. Here, use my phone to call Luis."

Five minutes later, a shaken Alberto rushed out of the elevator and onto the street, where he waved frantically for a cab. He hoped that his long absence from the bank had not been noticed.

But at the bank, his absence *had* been noticed. Bellini, Rossini, and Jim Daring were deep in conversation in Bellini's office when Mr. Rossini stopped and asked, "Where is Alberto?"

The vice president of the bank was a man of medium height with thick white hair and dark-rimmed glasses. He wore a dark-blue suit, and was looking at his watch, wondering what had taken the young man so long to return from his errand.

"Do you trust Alberto?" Jim Daring asked quietly.

Both men looked at him in surprise. Then they glanced at each other, as if waiting for the other to speak. Rossini hesitated, then spoke slowly.

"Well, actually, I've no reason not to trust him, Mr. Daring, but now that you mention it . . . " his voice trailed off.

"But what?" Bellini asked.

"Well," Rossini continued, "I don't want to cast doubts on a man without just cause. But in recent weeks, I have begun to have, shall I say, 'concerns' about Alberto."

"What kind of concerns?" Bellini asked.

But before he could explain, the secretary called on the intercom. "Alberto to see you, Mr. Bellini."

The three men looked at each other, and Bellini said, "Send him in."

Jim Daring was troubled. His mind flew back to the scene at lunch. He'd seen from Penny's face as Alberto had left the restaurant that she too was suspicious of the young man. Alberto had had the strangest expression as he'd watched Bellini read the letter he'd delivered—an expression that had not matched his answer when Bellini asked if he knew the contents of the letter.

But Jim Daring had nothing to go on but his own intuition—and Penny's. Mr. Daring knew that Penny had inherited from her mother sure instincts concerning people. They were not infallible, of course, but they were right often enough, and he'd learned to listen when his wife and his daughter expressed their intuitive judgment of others.

Jim Daring turned toward the window to ponder this matter as Alberto rushed into the room and began to answer Bellini's sharp questions. They were speaking Italian, which Jim Daring did not understand, so he was free to pursue his thoughts.

Alberto said in the restaurant that he didn't know what was in the letter, Daring reminded himself. *But when Bellini looked down at the letter, Alberto's face wore a sudden smile that seemed to indicate that he did know what it said! I'm sure of this!*

He was alarmed as he considered the implications of Bellini's remarks at the lunch table. He'd spoken of troubles for the bank, counterfeit money, and kidnapping. Puzzled, Mr. Daring frowned in concentration. A moment later, he heard Alberto leave, closing the door.

Jim Daring turned away from the window and again faced the two men, who both had frowns on their faces. Rossini spoke first.

"Mr. Daring, that young man did not have a good answer for his delay in returning to this office. What concerns us is the fact that three weeks ago, the head of our bank security ordered two of his men to keep an eye on Alberto. They've been doing this. And they just reported to us that after leaving the restaurant today, Alberto did not return directly to this office, as he'd been told to do."

"Where did he go?" Jim Daring asked quickly. Now his suspicions were being confirmed. His whole body was tense as he focused on Rossini's answer.

"To another office building in the city, a building our chief of security suspects is being used by those who are causing trouble for this bank. We believe these men to be a political action section of the socialists. They have caused our bank and our personnel trouble in the past."

Bellini was shocked. "Then Alberto may be working with those bandits!"

"That's a possibility," Rossini replied. "And one I think we must explore."

"But I'm concerned about the threat of kidnapping," Daring said to the two men. "Do you think that either one of you is in danger?"

"I don't think so," Rossini said slowly. "The socialists are trying to discredit the policies we stand for, and they can do more damage in other ways than by kidnapping one of us. It's our prime minister who's in greater danger. As a member of the board of directors of this bank, he'd be a bigger prize than either of us. No, I don't think that either Antony or I are in any danger. What we've got to do, however, is to stop them from flooding us with counterfeit bills."

Jim Daring began to relax. Perhaps these bankers were not in danger. He knew that kidnapping was a real threat in this country and that it had been practiced before. But Rossini should know if there was danger to himself and Bellini, and apparently he did not think that there was.

"Well, enough of these alarms," Rossini said, clapping his hands together as if to dismiss the threat. "We've spent enough time on that subject. Now let's get to the matter you brought before us, Mr. Daring. Antony and I are eager to do all that we can to arrange financing for your project in Egypt. Tell us what you need."

Bellini reached for his briefcase and pulled out a sheaf of papers. "Here's Jim's proposal. And here's how we can arrange our part of the financing."

Soon, the three men forgot Alberto and the troubles of the bank as they began to immerse themselves in the proposal Jim Daring had brought to them.

CHAPTER 4

THE PALATINE

"This is where Romulus and Remus were nursed by a wolf and raised to become the founders of Rome," David said as the three wandered through the pleasant ancient site called the Palatine.

"No kidding!" Mark replied, his blue eyes wide. "Did the Romans really believe *that?*"

"They sure did—for centuries!" David said with a grin. "That's part of their mythological history. It's myth, but they called it history, and they believed it. The legend says that the two boys, Romulus and Remus, lost their mother and were found by a she-wolf. The wolf nursed them and raised them in a cave right on this spot. The Romans worshipped this place for centuries. Right over there, in fact, are the remains of a village where people lived eight centuries before Christ. That's where the Romans believed Romulus and Remus grew up."

They studied the site for a few moments. As they did, they could not help noticing the two massive stone structures that dominated the whole area of the Palatine. Penny was busy with her camera, focusing on these, and she asked David what the buildings were.

Studying his guidebook, David answered, "Those are the Domus Flavia and the Augustana."

Mark rolled his eyes at the sound of the Latin words. "How about interpreting that for me, David," he said. "I'm a little rusty with my Latin place names."

"Sure," David agreed. "Those are the remains of a huge palace the Emperor Domitian built near the end of the first century. It was a monster of a palace. You can see from the remains how big the original must have been."

"I think I'm more impressed with the small house the Emperor Augustus lived in than with those huge buildings," Penny said. "Compared with that palace of Domitian, Augustus's house is so modest."

"It is," David agreed, "and that's interesting, because he was the dominant figure in Roman history. He's the emperor who rescued Roman society from the chaos of their civil wars and who pretended to restore the ancient forms of the Republic."

"The Republic?" Penny asked. "I thought Augustus had total power as the emperor."

"Actually, he did," David answered. "But he gave back the *form* of power and responsibility. He honored the Senate—Julius Caesar and his successors had despised the Senate—and his administration gave some freedoms to the aristocratic classes. So while he was actually in command, he exercised his power through the ancient republican forms of government. This made the Romans think that they had received their ancient liberties back. He insisted that his aim was to restore the old Roman Republic."

"But he really didn't do that?" Mark asked.

"No, he didn't," David said. "But he did bring order and stability. And Italy really needed that."

"Then he didn't do what George Washington did," Penny reflected, "because Washington really did give up his military power to the Congress as soon as the British army left the continent."

"Good point, Penny," Mark said. "That's why there aren't many men in history who can measure up to George Washington."

Penny stopped suddenly. "You boys stay there. I want to take your picture in front of that fountain."

Obediently, Mark and David stood where she directed and waited patiently while she framed her shot. Then she backed off a bit to take another. That's when Mark whispered to David.

"Hey, David, see that man just beyond Penny, behind that family of tourists? He's wearing a dark suit and dark glasses."

"Yeah," David replied. "So what?"

"He's been following us. Don't let him see you looking at him!"

David looked off to the left. "When did you first spot him?"

"Actually, I saw him earlier, before we went to lunch. But I didn't think anything of it until I saw him again, about 10 minutes ago. He's been looking at Penny a lot."

"Well, I do that," David said with a grin. "That just shows he's got good eyes."

Mark grinned in return. "Sure. But we trust you. I sure don't trust that guy."

"Well, let's keep our eyes open, then," David suggested,

alert now. He was frowning with concentration.

"Right," Mark agreed. "Let's get Penny and move on. I won't bother her about it unless we have to. Maybe it's nothing to worry about."

"Still, I think we'd better look natural and unconcerned," David said. "We'll see if he keeps trailing us."

Penny walked toward them happily, replacing her camera in its case and folding her light-blue raincoat again neatly over her arm. Mark suggested that they move over to the area of the ancient stadium. With Penny between the two boys, they walked across the grounds toward the sunken athletic arena.

"I've read about this place," she told them brightly. "They don't know if this was used for horse races or track events or what."

While Penny was speaking, Mark glanced over at the man who was following them. He was shocked to see that four other men had joined him. And the group was moving in the same direction as the Americans. Mark came to a quick decision.

"Let's head back," he said suddenly. "We want to be ready to meet Dad and Mr. Bellini when they come to pick us up. We'll stop at that outdoor restaurant and get something cold to drink."

Penny agreed at once. "Okay. It's hot and I'm thirsty." Then smiling up at David, she said, "Ready to go?"

"I sure am," he agreed, looking over her head at Mark. David knew at once that Mark sensed danger and that this was his signal to begin their retreat. He pointed and said, "That's the direct way to the street."

Penny noticed David frowning slightly, which he did when his mind was working on something. *Was something bothering him?* she wondered. She glanced quickly at her brother to see if his face showed signs of concern, too. But Mark's face was placid and pleasant, as it usually was. *I never can tell what he's thinking,* she reminded herself. *How can those two boys, who believe the same things, be so different?*

The three began to stroll in the direction David had pointed. Mark was on Penny's left side, and David was on her right. Both boys moved a couple of feet away from her and looked around casually as they conversed, so that at least one of them had an eye on the area behind.

"Wait a minute!" Penny exclaimed suddenly. She pointed to the ruins of a temple. "That would make a great picture!" She began to open the camera case that hung from her shoulder when Mark took her arm and kept her from stopping.

"Keep walking, Penny!" he said in a hushed voice.

She saw that his face was very serious, like David's.

"We've spotted a man who's been following us," Mark continued. "Some other guys just joined him, and they keep coming our way. We're heading for the entrance, and we want to keep ahead of them."

Her brown eyes widened in surprise. "But why would anyone be following us? We don't know *anybody* in this city!" She resisted the impulse to look back at the men.

"I don't know," Mark answered. "But that's what they seem to be doing. Let's get out of here!"

At that moment, David spotted a group of tourists some distance ahead of them, and his face brightened. "Hey, let's join those people over there. They seem to be going our way, and that should keep those guys away from us for a while."

"Good idea!" Mark said as they changed course and walked up the grassy slope toward the crowd of chattering tourists. As they came within hearing distance, David's face broke into a big grin. "They're speaking German!" he said excitedly.

David's family had lived in Germany for several years when he was young, and he'd learned to speak German then. When his family moved back to Alabama, his parents had seen to it that they all kept up their knowledge of the language. They'd listened to Germany's international news program on short-wave radio, and David had studied German each year since.

Mark and Penny, on the other hand, had grown up learning French. They too had been able to use this skill when the three had visited France before going to Germany.

As they approached the group of German tourists in the Palatine, David strained to pick up their conversation. Mark looked back at the huge ruins of the Augustana Palace, and as he did, he spotted the men who were following them. The men had drawn closer as the three Americans had started to leave the area but then dropped back when the Americans moved closer to the tourist group.

"This is great!" David said, his face breaking into a smile of genuine relief. "If these Germans keep going our way, they'll escort us right out of the place!"

Penny smiled bravely, but David could see the anxiety in her eyes. "It is a great idea to join that group," she said, "but I still can't imagine why anyone would be following us."

"Maybe they're pickpockets," David suggested. "I've read that Rome is full of them, and many are children. While one child asks you a question, the other steals your wallet or your purse or your camera!"

"I bet you're right," Mark agreed. "Come on. Let's get closer to the tourists."

There were eight in the party they'd joined. Half were adults, the others were children. David greeted them in German, and they responded with great friendliness. Soon he was busy answering their questions, which he interpreted for Mark and Penny.

"They're from Düsseldorf," he said. "I told them we visited there just a few weeks ago, and they were delighted. They'll be in Rome for several days, then they're going to Venice."

But suddenly the Germans bade them all farewell and turned aside.

"They want to see more of the Palatine," David said quietly, "so they're stopping here." Now his face wore that slight frown again.

Mark glanced around, pretending to be simply taking in the sights. His glance swept over the five men and passed on. He turned back to the other two. "Now that the Germans have left us, they're closing in again. But don't worry. They can't do anything while we're in the open."

Once again, David and Mark stepped a couple of yards away from Penny, keeping her between them. This gave the boys fighting room should any of those men attack them. The three walked more briskly now, yet they tried not to give the appearance that they were fleeing.

"I don't think they know we've noticed them," David said. "So let's just keep looking around like tourists do—and keep heading toward the exit."

They approached a group of pine trees and were about to head into the grove when Mark suggested they go around them. "Let's stay in the open," he said quietly. "We want to be in sight of other tourists."

So the three turned left and skirted the trees. Penny stumbled, and David reached out to steady her. As he did, he glanced back at their pursuers.

"They're still keeping their distance," he said. "I think we're pretty safe out in the open like this, in plain view of other sightseers."

Before long, the three saw a busy street ahead of them, and they all breathed a sigh of relief. They would be safe with so many people around. Happily, they walked out of the historic area and turned toward the restaurant where they'd had lunch. That's where they had arranged to meet Mr. Daring and Antony Bellini.

"Thank goodness we're out of there!" Penny said thankfully. "I was praying the whole time!"

"Me, too!" Mark said, grinning with relief.

"And so was I!" David added. "Wow, it sure feels good to get away from those men—whoever they were!"

He smiled at Penny, and she smiled back.

But just as they began to relax, there was a rush of pounding feet behind them.

CHAPTER 5

THE ATTACK

Mark and David whirled at once, just in time to drop to a karate stance and kick out at the men who rushed them. Totally surprised, the first two men lurched back. One fell down, gasping from the blow to his stomach. The other grabbed his leg, which had been kicked, and began to limp away frantically.

A third man ran toward Penny and lunged for the raincoat that was folded over her arm. She screamed, stepped back quickly, and grabbed the coat from her arm with her free hand. Then she whipped it across her attacker's face. The coat's belt buckle drew blood from his cheek, and he cried out as his hands flew to cover his face. Mark and David closed in at once and knocked the man to the ground.

The two boys started toward the remaining attacker, but he scrambled to his feet and sprinted away. Looking around quickly, Mark and David noticed that the man who had first followed them was nowhere to be seen.

"Hurry," Mark called as the two men on the ground tried to stand up. "Let's get out of here!"

The three Americans turned and raced away from the

scene, running along the sidewalk through a crowd of surprised pedestrians who parted to let them through.

They came to a corner and stopped. Here they turned and looked behind them.

"They're not following us," David said with obvious relief. His lean face was grave. "What was that all about?"

"I don't know," Mark said, unable to keep the concern from his face.

"That man grabbed for my raincoat," Penny told them, her brown eyes filled with worry. "Why do you think he wanted that?"

"Your raincoat? Are you sure? Maybe he was after your camera," David said. He and Mark had been facing the other attackers and hadn't seen the one who had rushed Penny.

"No, I'm positive he grabbed for my coat," she insisted. "And that doesn't make sense."

The three hurried across the street. But Penny's remarks had the two boys puzzled. Mark frowned and again asked if she was sure that the man had reached for her coat.

"I tell you, the man grabbed my coat!" she exclaimed, unable to keep the irritation out of her voice. "How many times do I have to tell you guys that?"

She was beginning to feel the effects of the attack now, and she trembled as she hurried to keep up with the two boys.

Mark put his strong arm around her shoulder. "Don't worry, Penny, those guys are history. They won't bother you now."

"I don't get it at all," David said, shaking his head. "With all those tourists in the Palatine—and all those purses and cameras and wallets to steal—they stalk us and then make a grab for your raincoat. That's crazy."

Penny's face clouded with another thought. "If I'd been alone, without you two, who knows what might have happened? I sure couldn't have stopped them from getting this raincoat."

"That's why you shouldn't be alone," David said, "especially not in a strange place. Many girls wouldn't get hurt if they only realized that." He glanced back again to make sure that the attackers were not following them and was relieved to see that they weren't.

"I didn't see that first guy," Mark observed, "the one I saw when we first got to the Palatine. What happened to him?"

"I didn't see him either," David replied, with a long, sober look at his friend. "But you're right, he was the one who was following us first, and he's got to be the one who sicced those guys on us."

They arrived back at the outdoor restaurant where they were to meet Mr. Daring and Mr. Bellini. The three stopped before a collection of round tables with red-checkered tablecloths, which filled the area between the street and the front of the restaurant. White chairs clustered around the tables, half of which were occupied by customers.

"Let's grab this table," David said, pulling out a chair for Penny and holding it as she sat. All three were alert and kept glancing around them.

A few minutes later, they began to relax again. The danger seemed to have passed. Mark pulled out his Italian phrase book and turned to the place he'd marked earlier that morning.

"My guidebook's got more information for restaurants, Mark," Penny volunteered. She reached into the pocket of her coat for her book.

"No need for that, sis," he replied. "My book's got all we need, and my innate gift for foreign languages has enabled me to master the phrases anyway. What we want is bottled mineral water and some pastries. You two just relax and admire an experienced tourist as I order what we want using the local language!" He smiled smugly.

"That's great," David said, rolling his eyes. "If we're depending on you to pronounce Italian, I guess we'll starve!"

But Penny didn't enter into their banter. She raised her head with a look of surprise in her eyes. "My guidebook's not here! There's a strange package instead—one I've never seen before! What's going on?"

"Oh, no!" Mark said in disbelief. "What kind of package?" he asked, leaning forward and lowering his voice.

"It looks like an ordinary business envelope—but several inches thick," she replied.

David slapped his hand on the table. "That explains the attack! That's what those men were after—that package in your coat! That's why they followed us and left those other tourists and their wallets and cameras alone!"

"But we have no idea what's in it," Penny reminded them. She started to pull out the package for them to inspect.

"Put that back in your coat pocket, Penny," Mark said quickly. "We don't know if those men are watching us, waiting for another chance to take it."

"That's *got* to be what those guys were after!" David said, excitement written all over his lean face.

Penny's eyes were wide with alarm as she shoved the package back into the pocket of her raincoat. "It sure must be valuable if four or five men were sent to get it back," she said. "But how did it get in my coat in the first place? It wasn't there this morning. I know I put the guidebook in this pocket."

"Good question," Mark said. "But the first thing we've got to do is keep our eyes open. We sure don't want to be jumped again."

"Let's adjust our chairs so we can see anyone coming from every angle," David suggested. The boys moved their chairs so that the three were now facing each other across the table. Each of them could see if anybody approached behind the other two.

"We'd better keep looking across the table and behind it," David advised, "until we figure out what to do."

Just then a white-coated waiter approached and in rapid Italian asked what the three would like. Mark looked up and in slow, careful phrases repeated what he'd memorized from the guidebook.

The waiter smiled. "Yes, sir," he said in perfect English, as he returned rapidly to the restaurant to place their order.

"Mark," Penny said, "you're a genius! Not only do you make the natives understand you, you also teach them English!"

"I told you I was mighty talented," Mark admitted with a grin. Then the smile left his face, and he frowned as he remembered their problem.

"Give me the coat, Penny," he said, reaching across the

table. She handed it to him, and he put it across his knee and put his left hand over it.

"You don't suppose those men would attack us again, do you?" Penny asked.

"Well, we're in a public place right now," Mark said confidently, "so we're certainly safe."

"I think you should call your dad and tell him what's happened," David said. "Maybe he and Mr. Bellini can come earlier than they'd planned and get us out of here before those men come back—or send others."

"That's a really good idea," Penny agreed. "Mark, do it right away."

"All right," he said, handing the folded raincoat to David and rising from his chair. "I'll try to find our waiter—or someone else who speaks English—to help me make the call."

He turned and walked inside the restaurant, and Penny and David looked at each other soberly.

"Let's keep looking around—just in case," he said. "We don't want to be surprised."

"David, what do you think all this means?" Penny asked.

Her hand held the strap of the camera case on the table in front of her. David reached over and covered her hand with his. "Beats me," he replied. "But don't worry. Your dad will be here soon, and he and Mr. Bellini will know what to do."

"I can hardly resist looking in the package," she said. "Maybe one of us could go inside the restaurant and open it. It might explain everything."

"You could be right, but I think it's too dangerous," David replied. "If those men would jump us in broad daylight, who knows what else they might do. Besides, what if one of them is inside the restaurant right now? I say let's wait for your dad and Mr. Bellini—I bet they'll want to go straight to the police."

In was warm that afternoon in Rome, but that didn't keep Penny from shivering. David squeezed her hand.

Mark came walking quickly up to the table and sat down. "The secretary said Dad and Mr. Bellini already left. They left early, in fact, but they're still planning to pick us up at 4:30."

"That means that we can't reach them until then," Penny observed anxiously, glancing at her watch. It was 4:00.

"I'm afraid it does," Mark agreed. "We'll just have to stay here and wait for them." His face was troubled, too.

"I'm not sure that's a good idea, Mark," she replied.

"I think she's right," David said suddenly. "If the guys chasing us spot us sitting here, they'll have over half an hour to plan an attack. Right now we're sitting ducks. Why don't we move around a bit? A moving target's harder to hit. If we keep walking around, they won't be able to spring anything on us so easily."

Mark frowned, his blue eyes thoughtful. "That's a good point. But we've got to stay in public view so they won't jump us again."

"That didn't stop them before," Penny reminded him.

"That's true," Mark admitted.

"Still," David said, "I think we're at least a little safer in a crowd of people."

Just then the waiter arrived with their drinks and desserts. To the man's surprise, Mark picked up the bill and paid him at once. "At least we can leave whenever we want now," he explained to David and Penny.

Penny took a long drink from the chilled mineral water, then said, "Boy, I was thirsty!"

"Me, too!" David agreed.

They relaxed then, as well as they were able, and began to enjoy themselves. But always they kept watch around them. When they'd finished eating, David spoke. "I think it's time to move."

"Where to?" Mark asked.

"We can walk a couple of blocks away from here, changing course as we do, so anyone following won't know which way we're heading next," David said. "But we'll keep close to this restaurant so we won't miss your dad when he comes."

"David, let me have the raincoat," Mark said suddenly. David handed it to him under the table, and Mark rested it again on his leg where it was out of sight from most of the people around them. Still looking at David, Mark fumbled in the pocket for the package. He took it out, slipped it into the pocket of his trousers, and handed the coat back to David. "You better carry this, not Penny," he said, his blue eyes grim.

"Right," David agreed, folding the coat loosely over his arm.

"Let's go!" Mark said, rising. "I put that package in my pocket so even if they get the coat from you, they won't get the package. We've got to give Mr. Bellini a chance to take this to the police."

The three began walking along the sidewalk.

"Let's stay away from the curb," David said, veering toward the storefronts. "We don't want to make it easy for someone to jump us from a passing car."

The three moved away from the curb, closer to the store-fronts, and walked briskly along. Penny was inside, closest to the store windows. She held her brother's strong arm. David walked behind them.

"If anyone wants to grab this coat from me, they can have it!" David said.

"Maybe someone will do just that," Mark said hopefully.

"Then they'll leave us alone for a while," Penny said, "at least until they search the pocket and find out they still don't have what they're after. This whole thing is crazy!"

"It sure is," her brother agreed, "but it's not the first crazy thing that's happened to us since David flew in from the States. Boy, has he gotten us in a lot of trouble!"

Mark tried to lighten the tension with this old joke between them, but no one smiled. They were too tense, too alert.

Soon they reached the corner. Mark and David looked around constantly, studying the crowds, searching for any suspicious signs from the people they passed.

"Let's go around this block," Mark suggested when they reached the corner.

They walked the length of the block and turned right.

"Let's wander back to that restaurant," David said, "so we can keep an eye out for Mr. Bellini's car. Penny, you look in the store windows, like a proper tourist, and we'll watch the crowds."

The boys also took turns looking behind them, pretending to glance at cars to their left or into the windows to their right.

Neither of them saw the green Fiat that had just turned the corner after them and had begun to cruise slowly behind. Inside the car, four men were fuming with anger. "I can't get you any closer than this," the burly driver insisted. "Those kids are sticking to the storefronts, and they're not coming close to the curb."

"You think I'm blind?" Luis snapped beside him. A stocky man in jeans and turtleneck sweater, he swore as he crushed his cigarette stub into the ashtray. "I can see what they're doing. I'd hoped we could jump out, grab that coat from the boy, and get away. Now I'm not so sure."

"We can't jump 'em here," said a man named Raoul from the backseat. "There are too many people on the sidewalks! We'd be recognized. Somebody in that crowd would get the license of this car and tell the police." Raoul was big, tall, and very uncomfortable in the backseat of the small car.

"But we've *got* to get that coat with the package," said Luigi, who sat beside Raoul. "Those are our orders. You know what the boss said!"

The driver was going as slowly as he could. Now he cursed as he was forced by traffic to speed up and pass the three Americans. "I'll stop at the end of the block, so they can catch up with us."

"Better not," said Luis. "Just let Luigi off at the corner, and go around the block. We can pick him up as we come back, and he can tell us which way they are walking. They can't go far on foot."

The driver agreed and pulled the car to a quick stop at the corner with a screech of brakes. Luigi jumped out, slammed the car door without looking back, and walked over to a book-store. He lit a cigarette and was pretending to study the books on display when Mark, Penny, and David came up. To Luigi's surprise, the three Americans slowed their pace, then stopped right beside him.

"Look!" David pointed. "There's a whole bunch of books on Portugal in that window!"

"Oh, David," Penny said, smiling up at him, forgetting their danger for a moment. "I hope we can go there. You really want to see that country, don't you?"

"You bet I do," David exclaimed, his eyes fastened on the books in the window. "I've been hoping we can go there ever since your dad said he might take us later this summer."

The three stepped closer to the store window.

"Well, you two take a look for a minute," Mark said with a forced grin. "I'll keep watch." He faced the street, then looked left and right at the people coming and going.

"How much longer before we meet Mr. Bellini and Dad?" Penny asked suddenly.

"Fifteen minutes," David replied, glancing at his watch. "Then we'll be okay."

Luigi stiffened at the mention of Bellini's name. *They're discussing their plans!* he thought. *What a break!* He contin-ued to stare into the bookstore window, hoping the Americans would tell him more about Bellini.

"Well, I'm really looking forward to visiting the Bellini's villa in the country this afternoon," Penny said to David. "Daddy says it's lovely there and that there are old Roman towers to explore."

Luigi's mind was in turmoil, wondering why it was taking so long for his companions to see their chance to grab the girl's coat before the three Americans moved away. He fumed at the thought that they might miss this golden opportunity. *Why, this would be easy! One of us could knock that blond boy down, the other could grab the coat that other kid is carrying, we could jump in the car, and get away in a hurry!*

Luigi winced suddenly, jerking his head back violently as the cigarette burned down to his lip. Cursing silently to himself, he tossed it away, and lit another. *If they'll just hurry and get here!*

He glanced back to his right, toward the corner. And there he saw the green Fiat turning in his direction. *Now we've got them,* he thought. *I'll just step to the curb and tell them the plan—one more man will be enough. We'll get this job done in a minute!*

His cruel face twisted into a sneer as he tossed his cigarette away. Turning sharply, he walked quickly to the curb and waved the Fiat to a halt.

Luis opened the window quickly, and Luigi leaned down to whisper his plan. Grinning, Luis turned his head and ordered Raoul to get out and join Luigi at once.

"Knock that blond boy down so Luigi can grab that coat from the other!" He turned back to Luigi. "Slug him first, Luigi."

"Gladly," Luigi said.

Raoul jumped out the back door of the car, smirking with anticipation, and the two thugs turned toward the three Americans.

CHAPTER 6

"DON'T LET THEM GET AWAY!"

"**M**aybe we'd better get back to the restaurant," Penny said, looking up at David. "Dad and Mr. Bellini might come early, and we wouldn't want to miss them."

"Good idea, Penny," David replied, turning away from the storefront.

Mark, standing behind them and still facing the curb, agreed. "In fact, let's go back and call again to see if the secretary has heard from them."

The three turned and began to walk toward the corner.

This sudden movement by the Americans threw Luigi and Raoul into confusion. Just a few feet from their target now, they saw the Americans move rapidly away from the waiting Fiat.

"What do we do?" Luigi whispered frantically. "They've gone too far from the car! We'd attract too much attention running after them, then running back to Luis. Someone might try to help them—or get our descriptions and the car's license number for the police!"

Both men hesitated, confusion written all over their faces as they looked back and forth between the retreating Americans and the Fiat. Luis, sitting beside the driver, saw the three teens walking away, and he almost went wild. Thrusting his arm through the open window, he waved violently to his two men, motioning them after the vanishing Americans. But they misunderstood his signal and thought he wanted them to come over to the car. They hurried over.

"Go after them!" Luis hissed frantically.

But it was two late. Luigi and Raoul turned to their left and scanned the crowd of people that had suddenly swarmed along the sidewalk. The three Americans were not in sight.

"I can't see them," Raoul said desperately to his boss.

Luis raged to himself, wishing he could shout at his men. But he restrained himself—they couldn't afford to attract attention to themselves at this stage. He swore, then got control of himself with great effort and snarled at the two men, "Get in! You've lost them!" Luis sank back in the car seat with a bleak expression on his face. How would he explain this failure to his boss?

Unaware of their narrow escape, Mark, Penny, and David walked rapidly along the sidewalk, weaving through the slower pedestrians. Mark glanced at his watch and grinned with relief. "Great! It's almost time for Dad and Mr. Bellini to meet us. They may even be there already."

Penny smiled and squeezed his arm as they hurried along. There were fewer people on the sidewalk now, and David stepped up to walk beside Penny.

"I feel a lot safer walking along here than I did sitting at that table," she said.

"So do I," Mark agreed. "David, you had a good idea—a moving target *is* harder to hit!"

"Thank the Lord no one's bothered us since we left the Palatine," David said gratefully.

They rounded the corner and in a few moments approached the tables outside the restaurant where they were to meet Mr. Daring and Mr. Bellini. Penny was the first to spot her father standing beside a table.

"There's Daddy!" she cried, breaking into a run. She rushed into his arms and hugged his neck.

"Hey, young lady, that's the kind of greeting I like!" He laughed, holding her tightly to his chest. He grinned at Mark and David as they rushed up but grew quickly serious as he saw the sober expressions on their faces. Instantly, Jim Daring was alert.

"What's the matter?" he asked quietly, still hugging Penny.

Mark quickly explained everything that had happened.

Deeply disturbed, Jim Daring took Penny's arm. "Here's Antony," he said, leading them to the car that had just pulled up to the curb. He opened the back door and motioned the kids in, then he climbed into the front seat beside Bellini.

"Let's get out of here, Antony!" Jim Daring said. "The kids ran into some trouble!"

Mr. Bellini's face showed his shock. "What kind of trouble?" He pulled away from the curb and the car moved swiftly into the traffic.

"Tell him," Jim Daring said.

The three told their story again. When they'd finished, Mr. Bellini asked Mark to show his father the package that had been put in Penny's coat. Mark handed it to his dad, who turned it over in his hand.

"It's wrapped up tight," Jim Daring said. "And it's thick but not heavy."

"Any name on it?" Bellini asked quickly.

"None," Jim Daring said, searching again.

"Well, we'll take it to the police," Bellini decided. "That must be what those men were after. We've got nothing else to go on."

Bellini steered rapidly through the city traffic and turned the car toward the police station. Several vehicles separated Bellini's sedan from the Fiat that followed him, so Bellini hadn't noticed he was being followed.

In the Fiat, Luis was speaking to his boss on the car phone. "Yes, sir, we've got them in sight. We know where they're going because Luigi heard the teenagers talk. They said that Bellini is taking them to his country estate for the night. Hold on a minute!" he said as Bellini's car turned right.

"Follow him!" Luis ordered the driver.

"Where's he going?" Raoul asked from the backseat. "That's not the way out of the city?"

"I don't know," Luis said. "But don't let him out of your sight." He spoke into the phone again. "Sir, Bellini has suddenly turned. We don't know where he's going, but we're following him. I'll call back in a few minutes." Clicking off the phone, he told his men, "Well, we know where he's going tonight at least. Now we'll find out why he's taking this detour."

In a few minutes, they discovered where Bellini was going.

"He's turning into the police station!" the driver cried.

"Pull over," Luis commanded.

The driver brought the Fiat to a sudden stop, throwing the men forward in their seats. They could see Bellini park the sedan. They also saw Bellini and the Americans get out of the car and hurry into the police station.

"This is terrible!" Luis hissed. "They must have found that package of counterfeit bills in the girl's coat pocket. And they're taking those bills to the police!" Luis was very pale now.

"Why did the boss change the plan, anyway?" Raoul asked sharply. "Those bills were supposed to be planted with the Americans. Then our men would call the police and have them arrested. They were going to blackmail Bellini and use him to create more trouble in the bank."

"Why were they doing that?" Luigi asked. "No one ever explained that to me."

Luis answered him. "The chairman of the board of that bank is a powerful supporter of the nation's prime minister. Our party's plan is to discredit the prime minister's chief supporters one by one, strip him of their protection, and destroy his influence. Blackmailing Bellini is a part of the plan. But now our leaders have decided to go straight to the prime minister himself. They planned to plant those counterfeit bills in his office. In fact, the police have already been tipped off. But we failed to get those bills back, and the plan is falling apart!"

"What a bungle!" Raoul said in disgust.

Luis twisted around and stared the man in the face. "I wouldn't say that out loud," he said in a menacing tone.

Raoul quailed under his stare and said nothing.

Awhile later, the four men saw Bellini and the Americans leave the police station and get in their car. Luis called his boss and was instructed to follow Bellini at a discreet distance. Luis replaced the receiver and spoke to the driver. "Keep them in sight, but don't get close." The Fiat pulled away from the curb and began to follow Bellini and the Americans.

Bellini was now in better spirits as he headed his car out of the city and toward his country estate. "How strange to find that package of counterfeit bills!" he said. "The largest denomination bills our Treasury prints, in fact! The police chief was delighted! He'll follow this up right away. Imagine, someone put them in Penny's coat pocket!" He shook his head at the peculiar turn of events.

Turning to look at Penny behind him, Jim Daring asked, "How do you suppose they did that?"

Her brown eyes were troubled as she thought. "I don't know, Daddy. I know that my guidebook was in my coat pocket before we left to tour the Colosseum in the morning, but in the afternoon, that package had replaced it."

"Someone must have substituted the money for your book when I put your coat in the checkroom of the restaurant," her father concluded. "If that's the only time you weren't holding on to it."

"But why? That's what I can't understand."

Neither could anyone else.

Then David asked the next logical question. "If they planted that money in Penny's coat pocket on purpose, why would they then try to get it back? That's hard to understand, too."

"It is indeed, David," Bellini said. "They must have changed their minds for some reason. Then they got desperate to retrieve what they had planted on you three." Then Bellini changed the subject. "Enough of this, my friends! Let the police handle the matter—that's their business. We're through with that money and those men who want it back. I want you to forget about all this and enjoy your visit to my country!"

The Americans began to be reassured by Mr. Bellini's confidence. Gradually, the sense of danger faded from the teenagers' minds. After a while, the car left the city and began to go deeper into the countryside. Bellini was a charming host, telling his guests of the great events that had occurred in this ancient land.

"Did you know that those hills once held the armies of Hannibal, one of the greatest generals of all time?" he asked. "Hannibal besieged the city of Rome temporarily but was never able to take it, even though he and his army stayed in Italy for 17 years. Every square foot of Italy has history lessons!

"See that subdivision?" he continued, pointing out the window. "Julius Caesar marched his legions through the land where those houses now stand when he led his army back from Germany. That's when he defeated his rivals and made himself ruler of Rome! Centuries later, the armies of the Gauls swept across that plain, crushing the Roman legions in their way, as they poured into the city to ravage it!"

"He puts me to shame!" David whispered to Penny and Mark. "I thought I knew something of the history of our country, but he knows more about every field around Rome than I know about all of America!"

"Don't forget, he's had a lifetime to study," Penny said. "You'll know that much when you're his age."

"I sure hope so," David said.

Finally, Bellini turned the car off the highway and drove through hills covered with trees. At length, they turned into the drive to Bellini's estate. They stopped at an iron-grilled gate set in a high stone wall. A guard stepped out of a small room built into the wall. He recognized Bellini at once and waved the car through.

"This reminds me of Mr. Braun's estate outside of Freiburg," Penny said thoughtfully.

"Let's hope that our stay here will be less exciting than the time we had there!" Mark replied quickly.

"Don't worry," David said. "This time we're going to have a real vacation!"

The green Fiat that had followed them from Rome did not turn into the road leading to Bellini's estate. Instead, it kept going another half mile, then pulled over under a cluster of trees beside the road. Luis picked up the phone and called headquarters for instructions. He listened for a few moments, then hung up.

He put the phone back and turned to his men, a broad smile on his face. "We're going to kidnap Bellini," he announced.

"When?" Raoul asked.

"Tomorrow," Luis replied.

CHAPTER 7

THE WATCHTOWER

Jim Daring leaned back in his chair. "Teresa, I couldn't eat another bite of this wonderful lunch! I doubt if even Mark could eat another bite after this feast you've given us!"

"Yes, he could," Penny assured him. "Mark's actually gotten worse since he's come to Italy. He could eat a lot more bites! I'm really worried about him." She pretended to look serious.

Mrs. Bellini laughed. "Mark, I'm glad you like what we've prepared, and you are welcome to enjoy as much of it as you like!" Mrs. Bellini was tall, almost the same height as her husband, with long black hair streaked with gray. She'd welcomed Jim Daring and the teenagers with great enthusiasm the evening before, and she and Penny had hit it off at once.

"Thank you, ma'am," Mark replied. "I think I will." He reached for another of the hot, fresh rolls and began to spread butter and jam on it.

"Jim," Antony Bellini said, rising from the table with a smile of thanks to his wife, "let's go in my study and work on this project. We can fax our notes to my office, and they'll send us any information we may need. Actually, you and I can complete all our work while we're here. These young people have said that they would like to hike around the estate while we work, and there are some Roman ruins for them to explore."

"Fine, Antony," Jim Daring replied as he too stood. The Bellinis had seen at once that Mark was built like his father. Both had blond hair, both had powerful, well-muscled bodies, and both were in superb physical condition. "I think they covered a lot of ground this morning."

"We did," Mark replied. "We saw a lot."

"I think they're ready to climb that hill and explore the Roman tower now," Mrs. Bellini smiled.

"We'd sure like to do that, Mrs. Bellini!" Penny exclaimed. "I want to take lots of pictures."

"Fine, Penny. If you have a telephoto lens, you'll be able to get excellent pictures from the top of that hill. In fact," she added, turning to her husband, "you should lend them your big binoculars, Antony. There's so much for them to see from that height, especially if they climb the watchtower."

"I'll get them right away," he said, and he left the room.

"Let me give you a snack and something to drink for your hike," Mrs. Bellini said to the teenagers as they rose from the table. "Perhaps Mark could carry it in a pack, if I fixed it for him," she added with a twinkle in her eye.

"I'll be glad to, Mrs. Bellini," Mark said with a straight face. "I probably won't want anything myself, but David and Penny can't go far without eating, so it'll be good for me to have something to keep them alive."

Mrs. Bellini laughed and went to the kitchen.

Jim Daring smiled at the three. Then the smile faded from

his face. "You folks stay out of trouble now," he said. "Keep your eyes open. Antony says that you are certainly in no danger here—" He paused, then looked at the boys in turn. "But in light of yesterday's events, just stay alert. And keep Penny safe!"

"Don't worry, Dad," Mark replied, "we will. Besides, we'll be in sight of the house most of the time, Mr. Bellini told us. We can see that tower from the house."

"Fine," his father said. "But take the two-way radio with you. I'll keep mine in my pocket in case you want to call. In fact, I'll go get it right now."

A short while later, Mark, Penny, and David trooped out of the house and headed for the long hill on which the ancient ruins stood. "No one knows who originally built on that hill," Mrs. Bellini had told them. "The ruins are ancient. The Romans added rooms and built the tower above. It was used for many centuries."

The three crossed the lawn, let themselves through an iron gate in the hedge surrounding the grounds, and set their course for the ruins on the hill some distance away.

"It's warm," Penny observed. "But not as warm as it was in Rome yesterday. That's a break."

"The temperature really climbs in the city this month, my guidebook says," Mark replied. "This is a good time to be in the hills."

The slope got steeper and steeper as they climbed. Periodically, the three would turn and look behind them at the house receding in the distance and at the treed countryside beyond.

"This is a wonderful view!" Penny exclaimed. She wore her khaki slacks and a white shirt.

Mark was looking at the binoculars Mr. Bellini had loaned him. He'd taken them out of the case, which hung over his shoulder, and stopped occasionally to test them on distant objects. "These are great!" he exclaimed.

"What's their power?" David asked curiously. He wore khaki slacks and a blue T-shirt.

"Ten-by-fifty," Mark replied. "But you've got to have a strong arm and steady hand to handle glasses this heavy, David," Mark said with a straight face. "I think you'd better stick to those small compact binoculars you carry every-where. These would be too heavy for you."

David flashed a superior smile. "Let me know when you get tired of lugging them, and I'll carry them for you."

"Well, both you boys are about to lose all your strength," Penny said. "Do you realize how many times you have not lifted weights or practiced your karate this summer?"

"That's the truth!" Mark answered. "We've really gotten behind. I'm afraid David will be limping badly by the time we get back from climbing that hill."

David snorted. "We'll see who's limping. I just hope I don't have to carry you back!"

Both Mark and David had been training in karate for years. Their fathers, in fact, trained with them. But the teen-agers had been traveling so much this summer that they hadn't been able to practice as often as they would have liked. And they'd missed working out with their weights.

Moving on, they came to a place where large gray rocks

lay strewn like stones dropped from a giant's basket. The land dipped, and the house was no longer in sight.

"It's hotter in this gully!" Penny observed.

"I know what you're getting at," Mark said, "but it's too early to stop and tear into this snack! It's a good thing Mrs. Bellini entrusted this to me, or you two would have destroyed it by now!"

"Oh, don't be silly!" she replied. "If we weren't here, you would have stopped 20 minutes ago and eaten everything she gave us!"

"What did she give us?" David asked curiously.

"Let's see," Mark said, stopping to take the small pack off his shoulder.

Soon the three were sitting on the grass, drinking cold tea and eating a roll. "There's more for each of us," Mark said encouragingly, "and some chocolate cookies, apparently."

"Then we'll live till we get back to the house," David said gratefully.

Penny laughed. "David, you and I are hypocrites! All we do is tease Mark about being hungry all the time, yet here we are eating as fast as he is!"

"Sis," Mark said with a grin, "I'm so glad you finally see that!"

"Well, let's go," David said when they'd finished. "I want to see those ruins, especially that tower."

"Me, too," Penny said.

Finally, they reached the top of the long hill. Before them towered the remains of an ancient fort. The walls had been broken and lowered over time, the roof had fallen in centuries before, and loose rocks littered the ground all around. To the left was a tall tower, which looked even more ancient, yet it was more intact. That taller tower was the one they intended to enter.

"Boy!" Penny exclaimed. "This is great! Let me take some pictures from here with the telephoto lens before we go inside."

As she set her camera, David walked closer to the broken walls of the fort and Mark turned and focused his powerful binoculars on the Bellinis' house, which looked so far away.

"Man, think of the history that took place here!" David said thoughtfully. He walked to a huge gap in the wall and peered in. The ground inside was littered with stones of all sizes.

"Oh, this is splendid!" Penny said, her eyes shining. "You boys stand right over there and let me take your pictures."

Obediently, the boys moved where she pointed. She backed off and began to focus. Suddenly, David remembered the day before, and he whispered to Mark, "Hey, the last time she took our picture was in the Palatine, in Rome, and that's when you warned me about those guys who were following us. Hope nothing like that happens here!"

Mark laughed. "Not a chance! We're all safe at the Bellinis' place. Don't you remember that gate and the guard?"

"Sure. But like your dad said, we'll keep our eyes peeled, anyway."

CHAPTER 8

KIDNAPPED!

"Let's see what's in that watchtower," Mark said when Penny had taken their picture. "I want to try out these binoculars from there. Mrs. Bellini said we could see for miles from the top."

They walked over the stony ground to the tower and went through the opening in the wall where a door had been set long ago. Once inside the tower, they found themselves in a large room. It was without windows but had a stone stairway on the wall opposite the doorway through which they'd entered. Except for the light that spilled into the room from the entrance, the interior was dark.

"Be careful now!" Penny warned as David walked over to the stairs against the far wall. "Those stones might be loose."

"I'll be careful," David said, reaching into his pocket and bringing out his mini-flashlight and shining its beam on the stairway. "Let's go."

Penny followed David, and Mark came last. Slowly, they climbed the steep steps that took them to a second floor. Here they could look out windows on each side of the dark tower. And across the room, the stairs continued to the next level. Flashing the light ahead of him, David crossed the room and began to ascend the stairs. He turned the light back on the steps behind him frequently, so Penny and Mark could see where to put their feet. Carefully, the three moved upward into the tower.

They reached the next level and stepped into another dark, windowless room. A small amount of light filtered down from the stairwell above, but barely enough to see by.

"I'm sure glad I brought this flashlight," David said thankfully.

"Me, too!" Penny replied. "Watch your step, though. We don't want to fall into any holes."

"Okay," he said. "Let's keep going."

They began to ascend the steep steps to the next level. These stairs were steeper and more narrow. David held the flashlight in his left hand, and reached back for Penny's hand with his right as she climbed close behind him. Trailing the other two, Mark steadied himself with one hand on the wall as he climbed. They all noticed how their voices reverberated in the confined stone passageway. It gave them an eerie feeling.

Finally, they reached the top, and the three began to breathe more easily. They entered a small, square room with open windows on each side. David held Penny's hand as they crossed to the window opposite them, searching the floor carefully with the flashlight.

"The floor's okay," he said, shining the light around. "The only hole to worry about is the stairwell we came through."

"I'm glad to hear that!" Mark replied, stepping to the window beside David and his sister. "Wow! What a view!"

The binoculars hung in their case over his shoulder. Mark took them out, leaned on the window ledge, and focused the powerful instrument. "Look at that—we can see for miles!"

"Where is the house?" Penny asked, searching the tree-covered countryside before them.

A flock of birds swirled over the gully through which they had come a few minutes before, and thick, white clouds hung in the sky above.

"Out this way," David answered, stepping to the window to their right. "That's where we came from."

Penny moved over to join David. She took out her camera and began to look through the telephoto lens while David withdrew his compact binoculars from the case on his belt and peered through those. Mark was still searching the countryside with the powerful glasses their host had loaned him.

"There's the house," Penny said at last, finally locating it through her telephoto lens. "Boy, we've come a long way!"

"But things look like they're right next door through these!" Mark said, walking over to Penny and holding out Bellini's binoculars. "Take a look."

She handed him her camera, took the heavy binoculars he gave her, and began to focus them on the distance. "Wow!" she said, awed at the view through the lenses. "You're right. And I can see the road that brought us to the house. And the hills beyond."

She gave him back the binoculars and began to take pictures with her camera. The boys moved along the wall, awed at the vista before and below them. The land sloped away from the hill on which the tall tower stood, giving them all a view for miles. Clusters of trees dotted the hills. Jagged out-croppings of rock pushed up from the ground in places. On distant hills, small dots became houses and villas when the boys looked through the binoculars.

"If the ancient Romans had only had binoculars like these," Mark said, "they could have done some real scouting from this tower."

Suddenly, a buzz sounded from the pack that Mark had taken from his back and set on the floor. "That must be Dad," Mark said, as he crossed the room and took out the compact two-way radio. "Mark here," he said.

His father's strong voice came to them. "How are you three doing?"

"Great, Dad!" Mark replied. "We're at the top of the tower, and we can see for miles."

"Fine," Jim Daring replied, "then you'll be able to see Mr. Bellini and me leave the house in a minute and drive to visit a friend of his. We'll be back in about an hour."

"Okay, Dad," Mark answered. "Take your time. We've got lots to do and see here."

"Excellent," his dad replied. "Just keep your eyes open and take good care of Penny."

"Sure will," he said. "We'll see you later."

Mark put the radio back in the pack and stepped to the window that faced the direction of the Bellinis' house. "I'll see if I can watch them leave," he said as he looked through the big binoculars.

Soon he saw the car drive away from the house. "There they go," Mark observed.

He followed the vehicle as it descended the winding road. It reached the gate, turned right, and headed down the road.

As he drove away from his home, Antony Bellini began to tell Jim Daring about some of the other estates in the area.

"That property to your right, Jim, adjoins mine and belongs to an Italian family that's been here for years and years. Their ancestors reach back into our country's history. In fact, the place has been in their family for several hundred years."

Mr. Daring studied the landscape Bellini described, but couldn't see the houses because of the thick trees.

They'd driven another quarter of a mile when Jim Daring asked his host, "What's that estate on the left, the one that slopes up that steep hill?"

"That's got a history, too," Bellini replied. "It's centuries old. The main house has been completely redone by the new owners. A good friend of mine owned it for years—he inherited it from his father—and Teresa and I have spent many pleasant hours visiting the place. But they sold it just a year ago."

"Who bought it?" Jim Daring asked. The place began to hold a curious fascination for him, and he didn't know why.

"Someone from Sicily. But the man's a recluse. He's made no friends around here, it seems. Cars drive in periodically, but no one knows who they are or where they come from. It's strange, really. Teresa thinks that the man is up to no good." He laughed and added, "But she's inclined to be suspicious."

They drove past the entrance to the Sicilian's estate, and Mr. Daring still found himself intrigued by the place. He spotted houses far up the hill, and when they had gone another quarter of a mile, he noticed a narrow dirt road leading up the hill toward the back part of the property.

High in the tower and far from the car Mr. Bellini and Jim Daring were riding in, Mark followed them with the powerful binoculars. "I can still see their car," Mark said. "These glasses are terrific! Now two cars are about to pass them." Suddenly, he stiffened. "Hey! What's going on?"

"What's the matter?" Penny said as she and David moved to his side.

"Those other cars forced Mr. Bellini's car off the road!" Mark said in a shocked voice.

Just then, the radio buzzed. "I'll get that," David said quickly. "You keep watching!" Reaching down to Mark's pack on the floor, David took out the radio. "Yes, sir. What's happening?"

"Two cars shoved us to the side of the road!" Jim Daring's voice replied evenly. "Several men are walking toward us. Here's the license number of the car ahead. I'll stick this radio in my pocket and hope they don't find it for a while, so you can hear what goes on. Listen closely. Then get back to the house and call the police."

"Yes, sir!" David said quietly.

Swiftly, Mr. Daring called out the license number of the car ahead. Then he stopped talking.

Horrified, the teenagers heard through the radio the sound of the car's doors opening. They listened as a man spoke to Bellini in rapid Italian. Their host answered, his voice steady.

"They're making Dad and Mr. Bellini get into the second car," Mark said grimly, his eyes glued to the binoculars. "One of those men just got in Mr. Bellini's car."

Through the radio, the three heard car doors slam shut and the sounds of a car's engine. Mark saw the three cars turn around, then head back the way they had come. In agonizing suspense, the three strained to hear what they could from Jim Daring's radio, as Mark kept track of the cars through the binoculars.

He saw them drive back past the narrow dirt road that Mr. Bellini's car had passed just a few moments before. Then he saw the cars reach the main driveway leading to the estate. Suddenly, they turned right, and began to drive up the hill to a cluster of houses above them. Mark didn't know that this was the same estate Bellini had been describing to Jim Daring, the one that had fascinated Daring as they'd driven past it just a few moments before.

"This is horrible!" Penny cried, tears in her eyes. "What are we going to do?"

"Just a minute, sis," Mark said, his voice shaking. "Let me see if I can spot which building they're taking Dad to."

Through the two-way radio came brief snatches of conversation, but it was all in Italian and they couldn't understand any of it.

"I can still see those cars!" Mark said. "They're going past a large house. Now they're parking beside a smaller building behind it. Hey, they're not far from Mr. Bellini's house at all —just across the valley, almost."

"But they're prisoners!" David said grimly.

CHAPTER 9

"WE'VE GOT TO CALL THE POLICE!"

On the top floor of the ancient Roman tower, Mark, Penny, and David looked at each other with anguish in their eyes. Mark was the first to speak.

"David, I think you and Penny should get back to the villa as fast as you can and call the police. I'll stay here to keep watching the house where Dad and Mr. Bellini are being held. If they take them away from there, I will at least know which direction they head. And we've got one license number for the police already."

David hesitated, a frown on his face. "I hate for us to separate," he said.

"So do I, Mark," Penny added. "You know it's best for us all to stay together." She brushed the tears from her eyes.

"I know it is, Penny," Mark replied, his blue eyes showing his concern. "But this is the only way we can know if Dad and Mr. Bellini will be kept in that house or moved somewhere else. If I see them taken away, I'll run down to the villa as fast as I can."

"It'll take a while for us to get back to the house," David said. "How can you signal us if they take your dad away?"

"I've got my flashlight in the pack," Mark said. "If I see them put Dad and Mr. Bellini in a car, I'll see which way they go and flash you a signal in Morse code. I'll keep flashing till you signal me back, then I'll run down and join you."

"But how could we see your light in broad daylight?" Penny asked.

"I'll stand back in that dark room. I think you'll see it."

"We'll have to let you know somehow that we're ready to receive your signal," David said.

"Well, there'd be no mistaking a fire in the backyard," Mark replied. "Why not try that? Then I'll know when to start my message."

"All right," David said slowly. "Let's go, Penny. We've got to hurry."

"I hate to leave you here by yourself, Mark," Penny said.

"There's no danger here, Penny. It's Dad and Mr. Bellini who're in danger. I think this is the best way to rescue them. And I'll join you right away if I see them move Dad. You can start another fire when the police come. Then I'll know to come down."

"I'm so afraid for Daddy, Mark," she said.

Mark put his strong arm around her shoulder. She put her head on his chest as tears began to roll down her cheeks.

Mark continued, "But at least we know where he is, and we can get the police there right away—if they don't move him, that is." He turned to David and said, "You take the radio. I hope Dad can keep his hidden and tell us something when he has a chance."

"Okay," David said. "Let's pray that the Lord will guide

us and give us the right ideas—and that He'll get your dad and Mr. Bellini out of those people's hands." The three stood close together as David prayed.

Then David led Penny through the door of the tower to the stairway. "Watch these steps," he said, flashing his light so she could see where to put her feet. Carefully, the two began descending the narrow, steep passage, holding one hand against the stone wall to steady themselves.

They reached the ground at last. Emerging from the dark tower, they squinted against the bright sunlight but managed to walk quickly to the opening in the wall that surrounded the tower.

"Let's get down that hill as fast as we can," David said. "But be careful—we can't afford to sprain an ankle."

They began making their way down the steep, rocky path, avoiding loose stones that might cause them to trip. Two hundred yards from the top of the hill, David and Penny came to the shallow gully that seemed scooped out of the bare stone.

"We'll follow this again," David said. "That way, we'll be shielded from anyone who might see us. Not that I think anyone is looking, but we've got to be careful—your dad's depending on us."

Walking in the gully, they found it easier to move swiftly since there were fewer loose stones littering the ground there. They headed directly toward the Bellinis' villa, but they could no longer see the house because the sides of the gully sloped upward above them. Glancing behind him, however, David could easily spot the tower.

David held the radio in his hand as they walked. No noise

or conversation had come over the radio since they'd left the tower, but now the voice of Jim Daring came on.

"Can you hear me, Mark?" Daring asked in a whisper.

"This is David, Mr. Daring. And I can hear you. What's going on?"

"They've taken Bellini for questioning and put me in a small room attached to one of the outbuildings. They didn't search me or even take my wallet. So they didn't find this radio. Where's Mark?"

"He's at the top of the tower with Mr. Bellini's binoculars. He's watching the cars that brought you there. He can see the buildings where they've taken you. Penny and I are heading back to the house to call the police. Are you okay?"

Penny was greatly relieved that her father seemed to be all right.

"So far, so good," Mr. Daring replied, still whispering. "Bellini told me this is a political kidnapping, and I happened to be with him when it occurred. So chances are, we're not in any immediate danger. But you three have got to take care. We don't know whether you're safe now, especially since you can recognize the gang that attacked you yesterday."

Both David and Penny could detect the worry in Jim Daring's voice.

"Don't worry, sir. We're as alert as we can be. Mark is, too, and he'll join us as soon as we get the police or if he sees them take you away. He's watching through those powerful binoculars, and if they do drive you away, he'll see which direction you go. Then he'll run down the hill to the house so we can get that information to the police."

"Okay, David. I'll sign off now. Don't you call me. Someone might hear and take the radio away."

"I understand," David said.

"Fine," Mr. Daring whispered. "We'll see what the Lord intends in all of this. You all take care."

David stuck the small radio in his shirt pocket.

Penny's face showed her fear as she said, "Oh, David, do you think my dad will be okay?"

"He told me that Mr. Bellini thinks they're just temporary hostages and not in any immediate danger."

Then his mind jerked back to an immediate concern. "Let's stop a minute, Penny. I'll scout the area through my binoculars before we climb out of this gully. Just because we haven't seen anyone yet doesn't mean that no one's here."

"You mean someone working with the people who kidnapped Dad and Mr. Bellini?" she asked.

"Well, it's possible. Your dad warned us to be careful. We'd be dumb not to take precautions."

He took the compact binoculars from his pocket and climbed up the side of the gray stone gully. With his head barely above the level of the ground, he began to search the countryside. Then he climbed down and went to the other side and scrambled up to scan the area.

"I don't see anyone," he said, clambering down the slope to rejoin her. His lean face broke into an encouraging smile. "Let's go! The coast is clear on both sides."

"I'm glad you're being so cautious."

"Well, our dads taught Mark and me that we've got to be extra careful—and protective—of you and others who are close to us."

"I've had lots of reasons to be thankful for that this summer!" she said with a smile.

He looked at her for a moment. "So have I," he said, taking her hand. "Let's go!"

They resumed their rapid descent of the gully, searching left and right as they made their way toward the villa. Finally, the gully came to an end, and David stopped, took out his compact binoculars, and searched the countryside all around.

"I don't see anyone," he said.

They walked quickly, closing the distance to the house at a rapid rate. Suddenly, Penny stopped.

"What's the matter?" David said, stopping beside her.

"Oh, David. I just had the most awful thought!"

"What is it?" he asked.

"You remember when we were in Germany two weeks ago? At Mr. Braun's villa? And remember that some of Mr. Braun's security guards were actually in the plot to rob him?"

"I sure do," he replied. He looked at her soberly. "Do you think those kidnappers have some of their men in Mr. Bellini's staff? Is that what you're thinking?"

"Well, if any of Mr. Bellini's servants are working with those men who kidnapped him, then we might be walking into a trap. And if there really are some spies in his house, and if they capture us, we won't be able to call the police to rescue Daddy and Mr. Bellini."

"Penny! I never thought of that!" His lean face was grave at the thought.

"So what should we do?" she asked.

"Let's keep walking toward the house, just in case anyone's watching us, while we think about this," he said. "Besides the Bellinis' home, there's no other place we can go to call the police but the servants' quarters. Fortunately, there are three of those, so one of them should be empty."

"There's nothing else to do, is there?" Penny asked.

"I don't think so," he answered. "We've just got to pray that we'll find Mrs. Bellini and that we can call the police."

Hand in hand, the two walked closer and closer to the villa.

CHAPTER 10

"I'LL GET THAT BOY!"

The three men moved rapidly up the hill, approaching from the south, keeping low to the ground to stay out of sight of the tower.

"How did Luigi spot those people on the tower from such a distance?" Raoul asked, puffing and gasping because of the speed with which they'd made the climb.

"They've got a powerful telescope on the top of the house," Luis replied. "That's how they've kept watch on Bellini these last few days, and that's how they knew when he was leaving his villa. They've been searching this estate carefully and spotted those three people walking up the hill toward the Roman tower. They are the same American teenagers who had the counterfeit money we tried to get from them in the Palatine in Rome! We've got them trapped now!" His lips twisted into a cruel smile.

Antonio spoke then. "I just want to make them pay for the trouble they caused us! Those boys broke Giuseppe's ribs back in the Palatine."

"And that stocky boy kicked me to the ground!" Raoul said. "I'll make him pay for that."

"He's all yours," Luis replied. "But get down—there's the tower!"

They halted at once and dropped to the ground. Luis pulled small binoculars from his pocket and studied the tower. "I don't see anyone now."

"Search the windows," Raoul said.

"I have, but you can't see into those dark rooms, not unless someone's standing right at the window." Luis, an impatient man, cursed this complication. "We'll wait," he said finally. "If they're still there, we've got them trapped. If they're not there, then we'll know they've gone back to the house. We can get them later, when we're demanding the ransom for Bellini."

"That's not fast enough for me!" Raoul snarled. "I want to beat up that blond boy now!"

"You'll get your chance," Luis snapped. "But we've got to get closer and jump them before they see us. They won't argue with my pistol. Then we'll take them to the boss. But first, we make sure they're still in that tower."

High up on the tower, Mark peered through Mr. Bellini's powerful binoculars at the villa across the valley, unaware that three men were creeping toward him. He swept the yard with its outbuildings, the countryside around, then came back to the small structure where he'd seen the kidnappers put his father. Periodically, he monitored the progress of David and Penny as they walked rapidly toward Mr. Bellini's house.

Hey, he thought suddenly, *I'd better look around this tower, too! I've been too busy keeping an eye on Dad and*

Penny and David. I've got to make sure there's no one searching for me!

Realizing that he'd made a bad tactical mistake, he walked quickly to the other side of the platform and looked through the window. Seeing nothing suspicious, he started to turn to his left when movement on the ground below caught his eye. He stiffened, then kept turning his head as if he hadn't seen anything to alert him. *Was that a man's head behind that pile of rocks?* he thought. *I'd better act like I didn't see him!*

He leaned against the stone wall, in plain sight of anyone below, but turned his head to the right, lifted the binoculars to his eyes, and looked in the other direction. Mark took his time, then without turning back to the place where he'd seen the man hiding, he put down the binoculars and stared into the distance. His mind wrestled with this new problem.

Someone's working their way toward this tower, he reasoned. *Boy, was I dumb not to keep watch all around! Now to figure what to do. If that guy doesn't want to be seen, I'd better keep glancing around—just so I don't appear to spot him.* He began to do this, taking care not to stare at the spot where he'd seen the man. *I'd better look out from the other sides, too,* he realized.

Quickly, he crossed the stone floor and glanced over the stone, waist-high wall. *Nothing there,* he noted. He crossed to the other side. *And nothing here.* He sauntered back and leaned on the wall on the side where he'd seen the movement.

Below Mark, the three men breathed a sigh of relief.
"That was too close!" Luis said.

"I thought he'd seen us for sure," Raoul said. "But what difference does it make? He's trapped up there! So are his friends. They can't get away from us! Why not rush up and grab them now?" A powerfully built man, his jeans and turtle-neck shirt just barely fit his muscled frame.

"Because we didn't see his friends!" Luis snarled. "We don't know if they're there or not. If he sees us rush the tower, he might be able to signal them somehow, and they'll get away. We can't take stupid chances!"

The men lay low, behind a grassy rise that hid them from the view of anyone in the tower above.

Mark's mind was racing. *I've got to get out of here!* Quickly he crossed the room for a final look at the villa through the binoculars. He studied the building where his father was a prisoner. And as he did, he saw several men hurry from the main house to one of the parked cars and get in. He watched closely for his father or Mr. Bellini, but they were not among the men. The car left the house and drove down the long hill toward the main road. It turned and moved to Mark's left.

They're heading back to Rome! he thought. *That means there won't be as many men guarding Dad and Mr. Bellini when the police come.*

He crossed to the opposite side of the tower and searched the countryside, not letting his gaze linger on the spot where he'd seen the man hiding. Nothing moved, although Mark thought he saw the top of the man's head. *That guy still wants to stay hidden,* he realized. *Now, how can I use that to my advantage? I've got to get out of here before I'm trapped.*

Then his mind stopped at that thought. *I'm already*

trapped—unless I can get away before he gets to the door at the bottom of this tower!

On the ground below, Luis was peering at the tower through a thick patch of high grass. "He's still looking over this way," he told his companions. "But I don't think he's seen us. And I haven't heard any voices up there. Maybe he's alone." Luis thought for a minute, then made his decision. "We'll wait for him to move to the other side, then we'll go in. If he's alone, we'll get him. Then we'll make him tell us where the others are."

"I'll go first," Raoul added.

"There's no way he can get away from us now," Antonio hissed. "And his friends can't be far away. We'll get them, too."

Far away from the tower, Penny and David approached the Bellinis' villa with apprehension. Their minds had been wrestling with the problem of what to do when they reached the house.

"Here's what we'll do, Penny," David said finally. "We'll head straight for the house. But when we get close to the women's quarters, the one nearest to the house, you split off and go there. Knock to see if anyone's in. If they let you in, tell them what's happened, and have them call the police. And stay there."

"But what will you do, David?"

"I'll go to the main house and do the same. That way, if there are any of those kidnappers there, you at least will be able to get a call through to the police."

"What if someone in the house takes *you* prisoner?"

"Well, it wouldn't be for long if you call the police, Penny! That's the key to everything. If you can get the police here, then your dad and Mr. Bellini can be rescued, and I can, too. That's *if* there are any of those kidnappers in the house. We don't know, but we can't take chances—not after what happened at Herr Braun's villa two weeks ago."

"All right," she said reluctantly. "Let's go."

They came close to the villa and were almost even with the women's quarters. As they had planned, Penny turned, walked past the men's quarters, and headed directly for the stone building with the red tile roof where the female servants lived. She stepped to the door and knocked. Her heart was beating fast, and her thoughts were racing. *Will anyone come to the door? If they do, will they let me in? And will they believe my story and call the police?*

Penny longed to turn and look back at David, but she realized she shouldn't. She faced the door and waited. And waited.

CHAPTER 11

TRAPPED IN THE TOWER

There's no time to lose! Mark realized. In a quick glance, he'd spotted another man beside the first. Mark continued to lean against the stone parapet, hoping he appeared casual and unconcerned to those men hiding below. But his mind was racing and his heart was pounding. *I've got to get out of this tower before they come in on the ground level and trap me!*

Then he had an idea. He stepped across to the other side, the side toward the Bellinis' house and the valley, for a quick look at the ground below. Scanning the area, he saw a stretch of rough ground to the right. There were large clusters of rock all over the uneven ground, with plenty of places to hide. *If I can get to the ground, I might be able to escape through there and not be seen! But how do I get to the ground before those men decide to come in?*

He stepped back to the other side of the tower so the men watching could see him. *They seem to remain in hiding as long as I can be seen by them,* he realized. Leaning down, he picked up his small daypack from the floor and looked at the contents. His flashlight, two canteens of water, two cigarette lighters for emergency fires, and the remainder of the snack that Mrs. Bellini had prepared for them.

He took out the flashlight and the lighters, stuffed them in his pants pockets, and propped the pack on the edge of the wall, clearly visible to anyone below. Then he took out a sandwich, unwrapped it leisurely, and began to eat as if he hadn't a care in the world.

"Now he's eating!" Luis snarled, peering through the clump of high grass with his binoculars. The heat was getting to him now and sweat stained his denim shirt.

"We can't wait forever!" Raoul insisted impatiently, raising his head to look. He was getting hot and angry, too.

"I know that!" Luis hissed. "Duck!" he said suddenly as Mark turned his head in their direction.

Mark noticed the movement and knew he'd faked the men into ducking their heads. Then he moved to the door of the tower and started a rapid descent of the steep stairs, not daring to use the flashlight. He reached the third level, and then the second. There he crossed to the window that looked out on the valley and climbed onto the ledge. Lowering himself as far as he could, he dropped to the ground. He sprang up and began to run away from the tower, toward the jumbled piles of rocks he'd seen from the top. Swiftly and silently, he ran, covering the ground with long strides, praying he wouldn't make a false step.

He reached the piles of rocks and ran behind them, then continued to run downhill. The ground was steeper now and all his attention was focused on finding level spots to place his pounding feet. He covered 50 yards, 60, then 100. Glancing back at the tower, he could barely see the top. *I've got to get farther away! They could still see me if they got up there now!*

He dodged around a huge boulder, then another, running with great care, knowing that one false step would bring him crashing to the ground, perhaps with a broken ankle. *They'd catch me for sure if I couldn't run!*

On the hilltop above, Luis peered carefully through the clump of tall grass. "He's moved!"

Raoul could contain his impatience no longer. "Either you go up there or I do. We've waited long enough!" He glared at Luis.

"All right," Luis replied. "I'll see if he's come back." Raising his head slowly, he saw the pack on the wall. "His pack's still there, but he's moved to another side of the tower. Go ahead! Antonio and I will follow."

Raoul raised himself and sprinted toward the tower.

Two hundred yards away, on the other side of the hilltop, Mark came to the gully that David and Penny had taken a short while before. Leaping into it, he continued his run, breathing evenly, continuing to search the ground ahead for each step. Casting a swift glance behind, he could no longer see the tower! *I'm out of sight of the watchtower! Thank the Lord for that!*

But then another thought popped into his mind. *How long would it take those men to storm into the tower and notice me running for the Bellinis' house?*

At the villa, David walked to the door, his heart pounding. To his surprise, a frantic Mrs. Bellini opened the door at his knock.

"Our phones are out of order, David," she said. "My husband and Mr. Daring have gone to visit a friend! We can't even call our guard at the gate!"

Before he could answer, Penny came running toward him from the servants' quarters.

"The phones won't work!" she cried as she ran across the yard. "A maid told me they'd tried to call out, but the lines are dead!"

"Mrs. Bellini just told me," David said, more alarmed than ever.

"What can we do?" Mrs. Bellini asked. "And what does this mean? Oh, if only my husband were here!"

David's face showed his confusion. Finally, he blurted out, "Mrs. Bellini, Mark watched his car when he drove away. And he saw two cars make your husband pull off the road. Mark's dad called on his two-way radio and said they were being captured. Then Mark watched them get in those men's car and be taken back to that villa over there!" He pointed across the valley. "We know right where they are. Mark stayed at the tower to watch while we came to call the police."

"Kidnapped!" She burst into tears. "But how can we call the police if the phones will not work?"

At that moment they all heard the buzzer of the radio in David's pocket. He pulled it out, and they all listened breathlessly to Jim Daring's whispering voice.

"David!"

"Yes, sir," David whispered back.

Penny's eyes widened and she moved close to better hear her father's voice. Mrs. Bellini was suddenly still as she listened. She brushed the tears from her cheeks with her sleeve.

"Antony is back with me," Jim Daring said. "They questioned him about the large amount of counterfeit money that you all found in Penny's raincoat. He told them the truth— that we had taken it to the police. They said they're going to hold us here for several days. They said no one will suspect that we're being kept so close to the Bellinis' house. Some of their men have already gone back to Rome—Uh-oh! Someone's coming." He switched off.

"Oh, what shall we do?" Mrs. Bellini asked.

"Signal Mark," David said. "Now that we know your husband and Mr. Daring will be kept where they are for several days, we can call Mark to come and join us, then we'll plan what to do. I need to build a fire in the backyard—that's how we're going to signal Mark to hurry back here."

Quickly, Mrs. Bellini led them into the kitchen, where David gathered supplies to start a fire. Outside, he made a pile of newspapers and sticks, then poured on kerosene from the can Mrs. Bellini had given him. He lit a match and put it to the pile. As the paper began to burn, David turned his compact binoculars toward the tower, high on a hill in the distance.

"When Mark sees this fire," he explained, "he's going to step back into the room at the top of the tower and flash his light to let us know he's seen our signal. Mrs. Bellini, may we go to an upstairs room? It'll be easier to see his light if we're not in the sun."

"Certainly, David," she responded, "come with me."

She led them into the house and up the stairs to the second

floor. They followed her to a long, low room with two windows. When she opened the shutters, they could all see the hill topped by the tall watchtower.

Below them in the yard, smoke rose from the burning papers and sticks and curled into the air. Eagerly, David and Penny looked at the tower in the distance, waiting for Mark's signal. But none came.

"I don't see anything," Penny said with a catch in her voice. "Do you?"

"Not yet. Maybe he's looking in the other direction and hasn't seen it yet."

They continued to wait, and David again searched the hill through his binoculars.

"Oh, David, what could be taking him so long?" Penny asked in anguish.

"Maybe he's already left the tower," David answered. "That could be why he's not signaling. But just to be safe, let's build up our fire again."

In the backyard, they threw more sticks and newspapers on the fire, and the column of smoke continued to climb into the sky.

Up on the hill, the three men had rushed one at a time to the base of the tower and flattened themselves against the wall. Then Luis and Antonio followed Raoul into the dark room.

"Be quiet now," Luis hissed. "We want to get to him before he can throw anything down on us!"

"At least we know he's there," Antonio whispered. "His pack's still on the wall."

"Then let's go!" Raoul said. "And remember, that blond boy's mine!"

"He's yours," the leader agreed. "Just don't hurt him so bad he can't walk back to our car!"

Raoul turned and led the other two quietly toward the stairs. The three began to creep up the stone steps. They reached the first level and paused. Luis drew his pistol.

"It's empty," Raoul whispered, looking around.

"Let's go," Luis whispered at once.

Raoul led the way to the second level, and then the third, but the men found no one.

As they came to the top of the steps, Luis said, "He must be up there. Let's rush him!"

They raced across the stone floor of the room and out into the open area of the tower's top.

"He's gone!" Raoul said bitterly.

"How could he be gone?" Luis asked savagely. "We were watching the downstairs entrance all the time."

"Look over the sides," Antonio said. "Maybe he heard us and is hanging on to the wall."

The three fanned out, hurried to the different sides of the tower, and looked down the walls below.

"He's not here!" Raoul yelled in frustration.

"How could that boy escape?" Luis asked. "Go look below. Maybe we missed him in one of those rooms."

"I'll find him!" Raoul said viciously, rushing toward the stairs.

Luis and Antonio looked out over the walls again, searching frantically for the three Americans they'd been sent to capture. Luis took out his binoculars and began to scan the countryside around the Bellinis' villa.

Suddenly, the two men heard a frantic yell from below, then the sound of a crash. They rushed to the stairs and began the steep descent. On the second level, they found Raoul on the floor, twisting and moaning, his hands clutching his knee. Broken boards lay around him.

"What happened?" Luis asked, stunned at the sight of this bully writhing helplessly in pain.

For a moment, Raoul grimaced, unable to speak. Then, through gritted teeth, he replied, "I tripped when I took the last stair and crashed into this wooden frame, or whatever it is. It feels like I broke my knee!"

"Why do the toughest-talking men often scream the loudest when they're hurt?" Luis said sarcastically. "Join us when you can. We've got to find that boy!" He rushed down the next set of stairs, followed by Antonio. As the two raced out the entrance into the bright sunlight, they could hear the big man cursing them. They ran to the side of the tower facing the Bellinis' villa. Luis lifted his binoculars and searched the sloping countryside below, but he saw nothing. Then he focused on the villa, and he saw the smoke billowing from the fire.

"There's a fire in Bellini's yard," he exclaimed. "And a bunch of smoke! What's going on?"

"Do you see the blond kid or any of his friends?" Antonio asked. "They've got to be around here somewhere."

Through his binoculars, Luis surveyed the ground on the long slope that led back to the Bellinis' villa. "There he is!" he said excitedly. "He's running to the villa!"

"How did he get out of the tower?" Antonio asked. "We never saw him come out!"

"I don't know," Luis said. "He must have climbed down the wall."

"Not unless he's a spider, he didn't! There was nothing to hold on to!"

"Forget about that. We've got to figure out what to do now." Luis thought for a moment. "All right, we'll go back to the car as fast as we can, get to a phone, and call the boss. He'll explode when he learns that we didn't capture those Americans, but there's no sense trying to hide it from him."

"Our car is on the far edge of Bellini's land—at least a kilometer away," Antonio said. "We'd better get moving." Then he stopped and pointed back toward the tower, where Raoul was. "What about him?"

"Leave him. He'd just slow us down now."

As they ran toward the car, Luis said, "I wonder if that smoke and fire at Bellini's house was some kind of signal. We've got to tell the boss about this. He may need to move those prisoners."

"It's about to get dark!" Antonio observed. "See how close the sun is to those hills?"

"Run!" Luis said, increasing his speed.

CHAPTER 12

"WE'VE GOT TO RESCUE DAD!"

Standing beside David and Mrs. Bellini, Penny watched the column of smoke rise in the clear air. But she waited in vain for her brother to signal from the tower.

What's the matter? she thought. *Why doesn't Mark signal us?*

David was wondering the same thing. "I don't understand this," he said, a frown on his face. "Mark should be flashing a light by now. We were sure we'd be able to spot it from here."

"Perhaps the sunlight is too bright, David," Mrs. Bellini said, "and we just can't see his light. You said he had only a small flashlight."

"Yes, ma'am," he replied. "It's a small one. But I still think we should be able to see it if he stood in the back of that dark room. But I can't see anything! That's why I'm hoping he's already on the way."

Suddenly, Penny spotted someone running. "Wait a second! There he is! He's running down the hill!"

David and Mrs. Bellini looked up the hill and saw Mark dashing toward them.

"Here he is!" David shouted. "Thank the Lord!"

86

A few minutes later, Mark rushed through the back gate and into the yard.

Penny ran to him and threw her arms around his neck. "Oh, Mark, you're safe! We were so worried!"

"So was I," he answered breathlessly. "A couple of men were hiding outside the tower, and I think they were waiting for me to move out of their sight so they could come in and trap me."

"Did you recognize them?" David asked quickly.

"No. I didn't get a good look at them—just the tops of a couple of heads. They must have sneaked up while I was watching for Dad and Mr. Bellini. They tried to stay out of sight."

"How did you get away without running into them?" Penny asked.

He explained how he had tricked them into thinking he was still in the tower and ran back through the gully. Then he added, "I looked back a couple of times, but I didn't see them, so I don't know if they saw me or not."

"But what can we do now to rescue my husband and your father?" Mrs. Bellini asked.

"I've been thinking about that," David answered. "You and your servants should take different cars and go to your neighbors to use their phones to call the police."

She nodded in agreement.

"What happened to the phones here?" Mark asked in alarm.

"We don't know for sure," Mrs. Bellini replied. "We only know that they're dead."

"Those men who kidnapped Daddy and Mr. Bellini must have sabotaged them somehow," Penny said.

"You're probably right," David said, then he turned to Mrs. Bellini again. "You've got to drive somewhere to borrow a phone that works—no matter how far you have to go. We've got to call the police!"

"That's right!" Mark agreed. "There aren't many men guarding Dad and Mr. Bellini now. So now would be a good time to rescue them!"

"But it might take a long time if she can't find a phone that works," Penny said. "And those men might come back any time!"

"Penny's right," David agreed. "We've got to do something now, while Mrs. Bellini looks for a phone."

"I think we can," Mark said suddenly. "As I searched that villa where they're being held, I saw a narrow path that entered the grounds, way off to the right—a long way from the front drive. A lot of fencing material was piled up at the top of the hill. We could drive up the hill when the sun goes down— which won't be long now—and cross the grounds to the shed where Dad and Mr. Bellini are being held. We would come from a direction none of those men would expect."

"That's it!" David said excitedly. "Great idea."

"But that's so dangerous!" Mrs. Bellini protested. "What if you three were captured?"

"We've *got* to try!" Mark said. "We can't just wait here and do nothing! We'll be as careful as possible."

"We'll need some bigger flashlights," David said.

"And maybe a crowbar to force open the door where

they're being kept," Mark added.

"And we'll need a car," Penny reminded them.

"I guess you should try it," Mrs. Bellini said hesitantly. "But it will be dark in about 10 minutes now, and you won't want to drive with the lights on or they'll see you coming."

"That's a good point," Mark said, "though we may have a tough time driving up that hill along their fence line without lights."

"Not if one of us walks ahead in the path to lead the car," David countered.

"That's true," Mark agreed. "That would work—I hope!"

Five minutes later, two cars left the Bellinis' home. In the first were two of the Bellinis' servants; their orders were to turn right when they left the gate at the bottom of the hill, and drive until they found a house where the phone was working. From there they would call the police. Mrs. Bellini and her chauffeur were in the other car, and they turned in the opposite direction. They too were seeking a house with a working phone.

The sun had fallen beyond the hills in the distance, and the light was fading fast. As it became dark, a third car pulled out of the Bellinis' driveway and headed toward the gate at the bottom of the hill. David drove slowly and carefully, for he didn't dare turn on the lights.

From the seat beside David, Penny said, "I know it's tough to drive without lights, but if anyone is watching Mr. Bellini's house, they won't see us."

"That's right," Mark said. "By the way, have you heard anything from Dad on the radio?"

"Just once," Penny answered. "He said that they were okay but that the kidnappers would keep them for several days at least. We don't know what will happen after that, Mark. We've got to get them out!"

Just then, the two-way radio in David's pocket buzzed, startling them all. David pulled it out, flipped the switch, and handed it to Penny.

"Daddy?" she whispered anxiously.

"Hi, honey!" her father whispered back. "Where are you?"

"Oh, Daddy! We're driving—"

Mark reached forward and put his hand on her lips. He spoke into the radio. "How many men are guarding you, Dad?"

"We think just four. Antony heard several talking about going back to Rome, and then we heard a car drive off in a great rush. One of the guards is prowling around the yard and the buildings, but we think the rest are in the main house. Uh-oh—" Mr. Daring said suddenly, and the radio went dead.

"What happened?" David asked.

"I don't know!" she said frantically. "He just suddenly turned his radio off!"

"He must have heard somebody coming," Mark said. "Probably that guard who's patrolling the place."

"Oh, I hope that's all!" she said. "But I wanted to tell him that we were coming!"

"Probably better that you didn't!" David put in. "We don't know how secure these radios are. It's possible that they can listen in on your dad's calls."

As they passed through the gate to the Bellinis' estate and

continued down the road, David drove slowly, without lights, peering through the darkness ahead.

"You two help me stay on course," he said. "Penny, watch out your window for the side of the road. Mark, you watch to the left. Without the lights, it's real hard for me to see the edge."

In a few minutes, they had reached the main driveway that led to the villa where Jim Daring and Mr. Bellini were being held.

"That's the place," Mark observed grimly. "The house is out of sight behind that hill, but I recognize the entrance."

"How much farther till we get to the path you told us about?" David asked.

"I'd guess half a mile," Mark replied. "It may be the property line dividing their place from the next farm. I think I'll be able to recognize it because there's a thick clump of trees beside the road—and I think it'll keep us from being seen."

Carefully, David drove through the dark, holding the car to its lane with intense concentration. Penny watched out her open window for the side of the road, and Mark did the same to the left.

"Are you sure we haven't passed it already?" Penny asked.

"I'm pretty sure," Mark said. But now he was beginning to have doubts. *Will I be able to spot it?* he asked himself. *I've got to! We can't leave Dad and Mr. Bellini there! We've got to try to get them out while we still know where they are. If those kidnappers move them, we'll never find them!*

CHAPTER 13

STUMBLING IN THE DARK

"There it is!" Mark said suddenly. "That's the bunch of trees we're looking for. The road we want is right beside them."

"Great!" David said, relieved.

Slowly, David approached the trees, then he saw the dim outlines of the path. He turned onto it and braked the car to a stop.

For a moment, no one said anything. A great sense of their own danger came over them. They weren't sure how they were going to reach Mr. Daring and Mr. Bellini without encountering armed kidnappers.

"We'd better pray," Mark said quietly.

He prayed first, asking God to guide them, protect them, and help them release his dad and Mr. Bellini. Penny prayed next, then David.

They sat in silence for a moment and finally Mark said, "Let's go! It's time for me to get out. Don't run over me!"

Mark and David had agreed that Mark would lead the car up the hill on foot, since the road was narrow and it was almost completely dark by then.

"Don't worry," David reassured him. "Walk about 10

yards ahead of us. If we can't see you clearly enough for safety, I'll let you know. You may have to turn on that flashlight and point it at the ground behind you."

"You'd better hold your hand over most of it if you do," Penny said. "We don't want anyone on guard to see us."

"Right," Mark replied. "If I have to use it, I'll wrap my handkerchief around the light and aim it behind me. No one will see it but you. Besides, we can't see the lights from the house, so they probably can't see us either." He turned and began to walk ahead of them.

Slowly, David pressed the accelerator, and the car began to creep forward behind Mark. It seemed to David that he was driving into a dark tunnel.

"This won't work," David told Penny. He stuck his head out the car window. "We need the light, Mark."

"Okay," Mark replied, taking out the flashlight. He wrapped his handkerchief around it and turned it on, pointing it at the ground behind him.

"That's fine!" David said out the window.

Penny watched the dim form of her brother with increasing concern. "It's so hard to see," she said. "And he's not very far ahead of us, David. If he stumbles and falls, you'll have to stop in a hurry. Do you think we should drop back some more?"

David agreed and slowed to allow more room between the car and Mark.

The dirt path Mark walked on was rough, and he stumbled frequently. But he always regained his balance. *Boy, I could sure use that light in front of me!* he thought. The ground sloped upward, and it was covered with rocks and tree branches. He placed his feet carefully, ready to catch himself should he trip. *I just can't see what's on the ground! Oh, Lord, don't let me twist my ankle!* He could hear the low rumble of the car's engine behind him, and he hoped the sound didn't carry far.

Suddenly, his foot hit a branch, and he fell. Scrambling up at once, he continued walking, but at a slower pace.

David had braked the car when he saw the light go down. But when Mark got up, David pressed the accelerator and the car again began to move slowly after the bobbing signal ahead.

"Oh, David, it's so hard for him to see," Penny said. "Do you think we should tell him to use it for himself, and then flash it behind for us occasionally? He wouldn't stumble if he could see his way."

"Maybe he wouldn't, but the men in the villa might see his light if he aimed it ahead of him instead of back at us. Even if he's got it shaded, we just can't take a chance. Besides, if he aimed it anywhere else, I'd have a tough time keeping the car on the path. Let's keep doing what we're doing. Hopefully, we won't have much farther to go."

But David was wrong. There was a long way to go to reach the pile of fencing that Mark had seen through the binoculars from the watchtower.

David glanced periodically to his left, in the direction of the villa where they were heading. Suddenly, he saw lights in the distance.

"I see the lights of their buildings!" he said, alarm in his voice.

Penny could barely make out the lights in the distance. "Looks like we're still a long way off," she said.

Ahead of the car, Mark found that the road was getting even worse. Suddenly, he fell again. He scrambled up and moved on. But he'd hurt his knee this time, and he was disgusted with himself for such a clumsy fall. *I've got to land better than that!* he thought. *I can't injure myself now and leave this job to David and Penny!*

"Maybe I should change places with him," David said to Penny. He leaned out the window and called to Mark. When Mark walked back to the car, David offered to swap places.

"Thanks, anyway," Mark said. "But this road takes some getting used to—and driving that car on it does, too! Let's stick to what we're doing. We might be halfway there already."

Mark walked ahead again as David trailed him in the car.

"I think he usually takes the hardest jobs," David said quietly.

"I don't think so," Penny replied at once. "David, you both try to do that and make it easier for the other! I think it's very even."

David didn't reply. He thought often of Mark's courage and willingness to shoulder responsibilities—and more than his share of responsibilities, if need be. David had been raised with the same sense of duty, and it bothered him that Mark might be taking on more of the tough work in all the adventures they encountered. *But there's nothing I can do about it now,* he realized. *And he's right about driving the car in the dark on this road—it's not easy. I guess we better stick to what we're doing.*

Far away, in the securely locked shed, Jim Daring and Mr. Bellini listened to a guard walk past. When he had left, Bellini whispered, "Think we should call the kids again?"

"Yes," Jim Daring replied. "I'll see if they've learned anything. Maybe the police are almost here."

He pulled the two-way radio from the pocket of his trousers, turned it on, and whispered into it, "Penny."

Penny gave a soft cry when she heard her father's voice coming over the radio. "Yes?" she whispered. "I'm here!"

"Hi, honey! How are you doing?"

"We're fine, Daddy, but how are *you* doing?"

"We're okay, Penny. The guard just walked past a minute ago. Sometimes we can hear the door open from the house— it's about 50 feet from us. But that's all that's happening. The place is quiet now that those men left. Do you know when the police will arrive?"

"No, I don't. There's been a problem. We were about to tell you the last time you called, but you stopped talking. The phones in Mr. Bellini's house were all out of order. We think they were sabotaged somehow. Mrs. Bellini and some servants are trying to find a phone that works so they can call the police. But we don't know if they have or not."

"Where are you?" her dad asked, alarmed at the news.

David reached over and touched her shoulder. "Talk to him in Swahili, Penny! Just in case someone's listening in."

Startled, she paused for a moment.

Her father asked more urgently this time, "Penny, where are you?"

Speaking the East African language she and her family

knew so well, she said, "We're in a car at the far edge of the property where you've been taken, Daddy. Mark's walking ahead of us with the flashlight to show the way. David's driving. The boys are going to go to the shed and get you out!"

"What?" her father replied, also in Swahili. "Tell them I don't want them to take any chances with your safety, Penny!"

"But the police might not get here for a long time," she replied. "If the people who kidnapped you find out that Mrs. Bellini is trying to call the police, they might move you—and we'd never know where. Mark and David won't let me get into danger. But they think they can sneak up to the shed and get you out!"

"But there's a guard walking around all the time."

"I know, but they'll look out for him—and get to you after he's gone past. Just a minute, let me tell David what we're saying."

Quickly, she told him of her father's concern.

David replied, "Tell him—in Swahili—that we're going to leave you at the wheel of the car, locked in, ready to drive off at the first sign of danger. Mark and I will sneak up to the villa. We hope we can break them out, get back to the road, and jump in the car. Then you'll drive us out of here."

She relayed this to her father in Swahili. For the hundredth time, David wished he'd taken some time in the summer to learn a bit of that language. After a few more words, her father, sounding deeply troubled, signed off.

Penny put down the radio and turned to David. "He's worried about us coming after him!"

"So am I," David admitted. "But we'll make sure you're

locked in the car and ready to go. And there's probably only four men guarding them—and they don't know we're coming. Besides, if we don't get them out before those kidnappers move them, the police might never find out where they are. I don't know what else to do, Penny!"

"Neither do I," she said. "I think we're doing the right thing."

She and David concentrated on the bobbing light ahead of them, as Mark picked his way carefully through the darkness and the treacherous rutted road.

CHAPTER 14

PENNY ALONE

Mark fell again, scraping his other knee. Both knees were bleeding now. He got up, more slowly this time, swayed a little, then moved on. As usual, David had stopped the moment he'd seen Mark's light go down.

"David, it's taking him longer to get moving again," Penny said in a low tone.

"I'll tell him he's got to trade places with me!" David replied quietly.

David leaned out the window and was about to call to Mark when the light waved frantically. David stopped the car at once.

In a moment, Mark was leaning against the door, whispering excitedly, "We made it! We've reached that pile of fencing! I can't see the lights, so that means the hill hides us from the house."

"Great!" David said. "Now, scout the ground on both sides of the road and tell me where I can back up and turn around."

"Right." Mark moved ahead and turned the flashlight toward the ground, sweeping to his left. He walked around in a large circle, peering intently at the ground, then returned to David.

"You won't have to back up at all. Just turn to the left and make a circle. I'll lead you back to the road so the car will be pointing downhill and ready to go. These trees will hide the car. Follow me."

David turned the wheel as he pressed the accelerator. Slowly, the car bumped over the rough ground, swinging around, following Mark's light. A moment later, David had the car back on the rocky path. He put the car in park and turned off the engine.

"Okay, Penny," he said. "Slide over and take the wheel."

David got out, closing the door as quietly as he could.

"Mark, are you hurt?" Penny asked as Mark came to stand beside the car.

"Just scraped up a bit," his cheerful voice replied. "But I'm glad that part's over."

"Yeah, but the next part won't be easy!" David said.

"I know," Mark replied, "but at least I won't have a car breathing down my back anymore! Have you got the crow-bar?"

"I've got it," David said. "Let's go over our plan."

They huddled beside the car.

"Okay," David continued, "Penny will stay in the car—all ready to go when we get back with your father and Mr. Bellini. I'm not sure exactly what direction the shed is from here, but we'll try to approach from in front of you, Penny. Watch for our flashlight signal. When you see me flash the light four times, start the car, and come get us."

"But be ready to take off if anyone else comes first!" Mark emphasized. "If they find you before we get back, drive down the path to the highway and go for help!"

"I will," she said. "But I sure hate to think of leaving you two in danger!"

"I do, too, and I hope you won't have to," Mark said.

"We'll be as careful as we can, Penny," David assured her. Then he said to Mark, "Okay, let's head for the villa. We should be able to spot the lights as soon as we top that hill."

"And I know which shed those men put Dad and Mr. Bellini in," Mark added.

"Don't forget the guard," Penny warned.

"Don't worry!" Mark replied. "We'll sneak as close as we can, wait for him to pass, then get to the shed and use the crowbar to open the door."

Mark turned to David. "Let's call Dad. I think we can risk it. If anyone hears, they won't know where we are. We want them to be ready to make a break for it when we get to the shed."

"I think you boys should keep the radio," she said, handing it to Mark. "You might need to hear from Daddy if he calls. And you can tell him exactly when you're about to break him out."

Mark took the small device and switched it on. Quietly, he whispered, "Dad!"

"Yes!" his father replied eagerly. "What's up, Mark?"

"We're on the way. Tell us anything we need to know."

"Nothing's changed," his father whispered. "The guard comes by every 10 minutes or so. As far as we know, he's the only one outside—the rest are all in the house. There are no dogs. Take care, Mark!"

"Yes, sir," Mark answered. He turned off the radio, then he reached out and touched Penny's cheek. "You be careful, sis. Get out in a hurry if anyone comes. Close the windows and lock up."

She nodded. "I will."

"Penny," David said, "like I said, we might be in a real hurry when we come back, so keep an eye out for us."

"Okay."

Mark and David walked off into the darkness.

Penny turned the ignition key partway and pressed the button to close the window. She flipped the switch that locked all the doors and then turned off the car's battery. She began to pray.

The boys reached the top of the small ridge and stopped. There, ahead of them, were the lights of the villa. Mark put into words what both of them were feeling.

"You know," he said, "we've never left Penny alone like this. But there was nothing else we could do."

"No, there wasn't—but that doesn't make it any easier," David answered. "At least she knows what to do if someone comes."

"I know," Mark said, "but it sure is hard to leave her."

David didn't say any more. He felt the same. They continued walking in the direction of the lights in the distance.

In the big house Mark and David were trekking toward, the phone rang. Alberto picked it up. Gone were the elegant manners of the expensively dressed messenger the Americans had met in the restaurant in Rome. Now the young man was clothed in dark trousers and a dark shirt, with a shoulder holster holding a heavy automatic slung under his left arm. The phone pressed to his ear, he listened intently for a few moments, then replaced the receiver.

Turning to Carlucci, he said, "Sir, that was Luis. He said that the American teenagers were gone before he and his men got there. They only saw one boy, but he escaped somehow. Raoul wrecked his leg climbing down the tower, and they left him so they could get this message to us as soon as possible."

"What? The Americans got away? Again? Those men of ours can't do anything we tell them! Where is Luis now?"

"He's at a restaurant, using their phone. He'll be here in a few minutes. But he thinks Mrs. Bellini may be trying to contact the police. A smoke signal was set in the backyard of their estate. Remember, sir, we saw two cars leave their gate through our telescope. Luis thinks we should consider moving those prisoners."

"Move the prisoners?" Carlucci exploded. He rose, tossed his cigarette across the room, and stormed over to the window, swearing. Alberto winced and kept silent. Finally, the big man got hold of himself.

"Luis really thinks Mrs. Bellini and those Americans might get to the police?"

"Yes, sir," Alberto replied. "And if there's any chance that the police might search this place, the time to move the prisoners is now."

Carlucci stood in silence for a minute. Finally, he made

his decision. "Maybe Luis is right. It's not worth taking a chance. Go guard the shed where the prisoners are kept while I tell the other men to pack up all our gear. We'll leave right away and put the prisoners in the other hideout."

Less than 100 yards from the shed where Jim Daring and Antony Bellini were imprisoned, Mark and David dropped to the ground and began to crawl. As dark as it was, they'd come close enough to distinguish the outbuildings from the main house. They had even seen the silhouette of the man patrolling the estate as he'd passed by the lighted windows of the house. Mark had timed the man's passage just before the two had begun to crawl. David was holding the crowbar in his right hand. .

Pausing for a moment, Mark checked the luminous dial of his watch. He reached out to tap David.

"That guard should pass by the shed in a couple of minutes," Mark whispered.

"Let's get a bit closer," David whispered back.

The two began to crawl again, moving with great care, taking pains not to make any noise. They scrambled over short, thick grass, evidence of a well-kept lawn. Slowly, they closed the distance to the shed.

"There he is!" Mark whispered as he grabbed David's arm.

David had also seen the guard's shadowy figure pass in front of the lights of the house.

The two boys waited breathlessly for the guard to move on. As soon as he'd passed the corner of the barn, David whispered, "Tell your dad that we're here!"

Mark spoke softly into the small radio. "Dad!"

"Yes?" his father's eager voice replied.

"Get ready!"

"Okay," Jim Daring said excitedly. "We'll be waiting."

He and Mr. Bellini had been sitting in the darkened room. Now they rose and moved slowly toward the door, feeling their way carefully in the blackness.

Suddenly, the front door of the main house flew open and light flooded the porch and the yard beyond. Alberto walked briskly toward the shed.

Just 40 yards from the shed, Mark and David froze in place and tried to blend into the ground. They were stranded in the open, with nothing to hide behind. If the man glanced their way, he would see them.

Inside the shed, Mr. Daring and Antony Bellini froze also. They'd heard the door open.

Is someone coming to the shed? Jim Daring thought wildly. *What about the boys? Will they be caught? If they're caught, we're all in jeopardy!*

CHAPTER 15

ESCAPE!

Mrs. Bellini was becoming desperate. She and her chauffeur, Mario, had stopped at three homes already, and in each place they'd been told the same thing—the phones were out of order.

"We've *got* to find a phone and call the police!" she told him frantically as they got into the car again and raced out of her friend's estate.

"Yes, but how far will we have to go to find a phone that's working?" he asked. The man had been with the Bellinis for more than 20 years and was heartsick at the realization that his beloved employer was being held by professional crooks.

"I wonder if the others have found a working phone?" she said. "They went in the opposite direction. Surely, those kidnappers can't black out all the telephones in the valley."

Soon, they came to a roadside store. Mario slammed on the brakes, and the car skidded to a stop. Mrs. Bellini jumped out, leaving the door open, and hurried into the store. She rushed to the pay phone on the wall—and it worked.

Thankfully, almost sinking to the floor in relief, she dialed the emergency number of the police. A moment later, she was blurting out her news to an officer at police headquarters.

As the word *kidnapped* spread through police headquarters, another officer came to the phone. Again, Mrs. Bellini explained what had happened and where her husband was being held.

"Please wait where you are, Mrs. Bellini," the man said calmly when she had finished. "I'll contact the chief at once, then get back in touch with you. Let me have the number of the phone you're using."

With tears in her eyes, she thanked him, read out the number, and hung up. Then she waited for him to call back. Mario came into the store, and she told him what the officer had said.

It seemed like a long time had passed before the phone rang. Eagerly, she snatched it up and found herself speaking to yet another officer.

"Mrs. Bellini, the police are on their way to your home. They will also surround the villa up the valley, where your husband and his friend are being held. Please remain where you are for now, and stay by the phone. We'll call you when it is safe for you to return home."

Close to the shed where Jim Daring and Antony Bellini were imprisoned, Mark and David lay flat, praying that the man who'd just rushed out of the main house wouldn't see them. The man did not look around but strode briskly to the shed where the prisoners were kept. Here he stopped, turned, and lit a cigarette. The boys saw the match flame in the dark, and in that moment, they each recognized Antonio.

"We can't move any closer or he'll see us!" David

whispered. "But we can't stay here either. If anyone else comes out of the house and sees us, we're doomed!"

Alberto turned suddenly, and the boys no longer saw the light of his cigarette. Instantly, David crouched and moved forward a few yards. Then, clutching the crowbar, he rushed the man. Mark leaped up and followed.

Alberto whirled at the sound of David's footsteps, whipping the gun out of his shoulder holster—but it was too late. David slammed the crowbar into his stomach, and Alberto crumpled to the ground.

Mark searched the front of the shed with his hands and found the padlocked chain that was looped through the door handles.

"David, here's the lock and the chain."

David reached for the chain, slid the crowbar behind it, and ripped it away. He grabbed the handle and pulled open the door.

"Let's go," he whispered urgently.

Jim Daring and Antony Bellini rushed out of the shed.

"Great work, boys!" Mr. Daring said.

"This way!" David replied. He turned and led the men hurriedly across the yard, with Mark right behind.

David knew he couldn't use the flashlight yet, not until they'd put the barn between them and anyone in the yard. So they had to slow their pace to avoid tripping in the darkness.

A second later, they heard a yell from the other side of the big house.

The door of the house banged open, and two men rushed into the light thrown from the open door, pistols in their hands.

A hundred yards away now, David still led at a fast walk. *I can't take a chance of running into something that I can't see in the dark!* he told himself.

The yells behind them faded as they covered another hundred yards, and then another.

At the house, wild confusion reigned. Luigi and two other men, with drawn guns, were sweeping the grounds with powerful flashlights, searching desperately for the escaped prisoners. Shouting his rage, Carlucci left the men, ran back into the house, and picked up the phone.

"Here's Alberto!" he heard one of his men yell.

But Carlucci paid no attention. Quickly, he spilled the news to his boss. "Sir, a gang of men attacked our guard and took the prisoners away! There's only one other road into this place—we're rushing to block it now. We'll catch them before they reach the highway!"

He slammed down the phone and raced out the door, yelling instructions to his men. "Get in your car, Luigi! We've got to block the roads. You two go with him," he said to the other men. "Block the road at the far end of the property. I'll follow you down to the gate and block the driveway. They'll be trapped if they're trying to get out by car!"

Carlucci ran for his car, and the other two raced for theirs. "Hurry!" he shouted, wrenching open the car door. "We can drive faster than they can run! We'll get them."

He jumped behind the wheel and turned the key. Gunning the engine, he backed the car wildly, turned, and waited for Luigi's sedan to pull ahead of him. Then he followed the car at a frantic pace as it careened down the long driveway.

Cursing and pounding the steering wheel, Carlucci pressed the accelerator, and his car sped close to the tail of Luigi's sedan. The two vehicles roared around a curve, picking up speed—hurtling straight toward the headlights of an approaching car that was racing up the hill toward the house.

Frantically, Luigi slammed on his brakes. The car charging toward him did the same. But it was too late. The vehicles skidded, then collided head-on in a gigantic wreck.

Luis and Antonio had returned.

The next second, Carlucci's car crashed into the rear of Luigi's shattered sedan. The battered vehicles rocked and shuddered as their engines died. Slowly, dazed men began struggling to open the doors of the three wrecked cars.

Still stunned, Carlucci shoved open his door and staggered to his feet. Stumbling forward, he passed Luigi's smashed sedan and reached for the door handle of Luis's car. Yelling wildly, he started to wrench open the door.

Too dazed to see Carlucci standing beside the car, Luis pushed on the door with all his might, knocking Carlucci to the ground. Luis staggered out, rocking on his feet, turned to say something to Antonio, then collapsed to the ground, landing heavily on Carlucci.

Beneath the man who had fallen on him, Carlucci screamed curses and pounded the dirt like a madman.

By this time, Antony Bellini and the three Americans were almost a quarter of a mile from the villa. David switched on his flashlight, scanned the ground ahead, then broke into a run. Mark and the two men started running as well. David shined the light on the ground behind him frequently, helping the others see. Running at an even pace, the four men covered the ground quickly.

At last, David could make out in the distance the dim outline of the cluster of trees where Penny would be waiting in the car. He angled right, directly toward the road, and the others followed. Coming over a hill, David skidded to a stop and hurried onto the rough path, where he turned to face the direction of the car. He aimed the light up the hill and flashed it four times.

Penny had been watching for this signal. At once, she started the car and drove down the rocky trail toward the waiting men. The sedan bounced over the uneven ground, but she kept it on the road. When she reached the men, she pulled to a quick stop, flicking the switch that unlocked the doors. The men piled into the car, Mr. Bellini in front beside her, and her dad and the boys in back.

"Great work, Penny!" Antony Bellini said. "Turn on the lights and make some speed!"

The doors slammed shut, and Penny hit the pedal, flipping on the headlights as the car gained momentum.

With intense concentration, she gripped the wheel and kept the car on the uneven path. The men tried to find their seat belts, but finally gave up—the car was bouncing too violently. Penny skidded the car around a curve, then brought it back on course. With her eyes riveted on the road, she sped down the hill as fast as she dared.

A sudden dip in the road threw the passengers around so

violently that Penny applied the brakes. The car skidded, then swerved back onto the path. Penny pressed the accelerator once more.

With every sense alert, she guided the careening car down the rugged path. One foot pressed the accelerator, the other hovered over the brake, ready to stop at once. For a moment, she had a frantic thought—*If Mark ever drove like this, I'd scream for him to stop!*

The thought vanished. They *had* to get away before the kidnappers could cut them off.

Mr. Bellini spoke suddenly. "You're doing great, Penny. Keep it up!"

As carefully as she could, Penny kept up the frantic pace.

Praying fervently, Jim Daring and the boys held on to the door handles and the seats in front of them—anything to keep from bouncing into the car roof above them.

Will we never reach the road? Penny wondered. Her hands ached because she was gripping the wheel so tightly.

Finally, they all saw ahead and to their right the lights of a rapidly approaching car.

"There's the highway!" Mr. Bellini cried.

"Is that car after us?" Mark asked sharply.

But the car passed them and disappeared behind the trees. They all breathed a sigh of relief.

"Careful now, Penny," Antony Bellini said. "We're about to get on the highway. When we do, turn left."

"But that's going *away* from your home, Mr. Bellini," David said.

"You're right, David," he replied. "But we don't want to

run into those kidnappers by driving back toward their gate. They just might be sending men to my house to capture us again. I think it's best to call the police as soon as we can."

Penny turned onto the highway as she'd been instructed.

"Drive fast, Penny!" Bellini said. "We've got to get out of here!"

The car shot ahead through the night, picking up speed.

"When we've gone 10 kilometers, if there's no one following us, pull over, and I'll change places with you." He patted her shoulder and turned toward the backseat. "Jim, you've raised quite a girl!"

"That's what we think, Antony," Daring replied warmly.

Then the men were silent again, not wanting to distract Penny.

For the first time in hours, they all began to relax.

"I think we made it, Dad," Mark said.

"I think so, Mark," Jim Daring replied. "We praise the Lord—and we thank you three! You all deserve a medal!"

"They do indeed, Jim," Antony Bellini put in.

The car drove rapidly through the darkness. After she'd gone 10 kilometers, Penny pulled over to the side of the road. She and Mr. Bellini changed places quickly. He stepped on the gas, and the car sped off again.

It was midnight before they returned to the Bellinis' house —and only after the police had told them it was safe.

CHAPTER 16

HOME

The teenagers slept late the next morning. Penny was the first to wander into the breakfast room. There, Mr. and Mrs. Bellini and her father were drinking coffee and talking over the events of the previous day. Jim Daring jumped up and gave his daughter a big hug.

"Hi, honey! How'd you sleep?"

"Great! Are the boys still conked out?"

"They seem to be," Antony Bellini said with a laugh.

Mrs. Bellini called for her maid and ordered breakfast for Penny. In a few minutes, Mark and David wandered into the room. Soon the three were eating while the Bellinis told them how the police had rounded up the kidnappers.

"I left to find a phone, remember?" she asked them. "But we drove a long time before we found one that worked."

"The police explained that to me," her husband interrupted her. "The counterfeiters had access to people in the phone company. They simply shut down most of the phone lines in the whole valley for a couple of hours so no one could report that Jim and I had been captured!"

"Well, I finally reached the police," Mrs. Bellini continued, "and reported what you had seen, Mark. They told me to stay where I was and wait for them to call back. It took forever, it seemed. But finally they called and told me that they had sent men to the estate where Antony and your father had been taken—and to our house as well. They told me I could return home, that they had officers there, and I would be safe."

Mr. Bellini picked up the story where his wife left off. "When the police chief arrived here—long after you had gone to bed—he explained the whole thing. That counterfeit ring I told you about has very powerful connections. They are an arm of a socialist group that wants to bring down our present government. Those counterfeit bills were placed in your coat by mistake, Penny, after the gang had changed their plans to implicate me. They decided to go for the prime minister himself."

Jim Daring took another swallow of coffee and set down his cup, anxious to fill in some details for the kids. "The men who had chased Mark from the Roman tower crashed head-on into the kidnappers who were trying to recapture us! They had a three-car smashup! Those men were in no condition to resist when the police got to them." His broad face broke into a grin, and his blue eyes sparkled. "What a reversal for them!"

"Remember Alberto, the young man who brought me the message in the restaurant?" Mr. Bellini asked grimly. "He's the man you knocked down outside the shed, David."

"Served him right, too!" Mrs. Bellini said indignantly. "Imagine, that young man working with those kidnappers!"

"And they found a man in the tower," Antony Bellini added. "He'd injured his knee when they tried to capture you,

Mark, and the others told the police about him."

"They almost got me there," Mark said with a shudder. "I wasn't looking around like I should have been. I just barely saw a man's head out of the corner of my eye. Otherwise, they'd have trapped me."

"The Lord protected us all yesterday," Jim Daring said thankfully. He reached over and took Penny's hand in his. "Sweetheart, I'll never cease to marvel at your courage last night, when you waited in the car by yourself!" Then, pretending to look stern, he added, "Nor will I ever allow you to drive like that again!"

They all laughed.

"Boy, that's the truth," Mark said. "I was scared out of my wits the whole time."

"Me, too," David agreed. "Penny, where'd you learn to drive like that?"

"You know I *never* drive like that!" she protested. "That was an emergency." She squeezed her father's hand.

"It was indeed," Antony Bellini laughed, "but you rose to the occasion, Penny, and drove like a professional."

"Kids," Jim Daring said, changing the subject, "we've had as much excitement as we need for a couple of days! We'll rest here today and enjoy this beautiful place, then head back to Rome in the morning. We'll fly out at noon, spend the night in Cairo with the Froedes, then fly back home to Africa the next day. How's that sound?"

"We're going home!" Penny exclaimed. "Oh, that's wonderful!"

"It's time we got back," her father said with a rueful smile.

"Our time in Europe hasn't been as peaceful as your mom and I thought it would be. But it sure has been profitable!" He grinned at Antony Bellini.

"It sure hasn't been dull, Mr. Daring," David said.

They all laughed at his obvious understatement.

But Mrs. Bellini frowned. "Jim, I hate to think that you encountered such danger visiting our home. You must come back again someday. Those counterfeiters and kidnappers are locked up now."

"We'd love to come back," Mr. Daring said warmly.

"Would you excuse us, please, Mrs. Bellini?" Penny asked. "We'd like to take pictures of your lovely home."

"Of course, Penny. Go right ahead."

The three rose, thanked their hostess for the meal, and walked out of the room and onto the patio. In the distance rose the hill they had climbed the day before, and on top of that stood the ancient Roman tower.

"It still stands guard," David said thoughtfully. "Wonder how many lives were saved by soldiers standing guard there through the centuries."

"No telling," Mark replied, "but it sure saved Dad and Mr. Bellini yesterday."

"Was it just yesterday we were standing on top of that?" Penny asked, her brown eyes puzzled for a moment. "Wow! Think of all that's happened since then!" She turned and went to her room to retrieve her camera.

Mark and David walked to the edge of the patio.

"I'll be glad to get home!" Mark said.

"Me, too," David replied. "Hey, you still haven't taken me

to that ancient temple in the mountains. Think we'll get a chance to explore that?"

"Sure we will," Mark said. "Dad told me that there's a level field just a few hundred yards from the ruins. He's landed there, in fact. The jungle's covered the buildings for so long that no one knew it was there. People just discovered it last year, and no one goes there yet. We'll have the place to ourselves!"

"Unless we run into Hoffmann!" David said with a straight face, referring to their old nemesis, who had threatened their lives several times.

"Let's have no talk about that man!" Penny said, coming up behind the two. "That's one guy I want to forget!"

The boys laughed. "Well, there's no likelihood he'll go back to Africa now," David said. "The police are looking for him, remember? I think we're through with him."

"Where now, Penny?" Mark asked. "You be the famous photographer. We'll be your film-bearers!"

"As long as we don't let her drive, Mark," David said.

"Right," Mark agreed. "As long as we don't let her drive."

She laughed, and the three began to explore the grounds of the lovely estate.

Awesome Adventures with the Daring Family!

Everywhere Mark and Penny Daring and their friend David go, there's sure to be lots of action, mystery and suspense! Join them on each of their unpredictable, faith-building voyages in the "Daring Adventure" series as they learn to rely on each other and—most importantly—God!

Ambushed in Africa (#1)
An attempted kidnapping! A daring rescue! A breathtaking chase through crocodile-infested waters! Can the trio outwit the criminals before the top secret African diamond mine surveys are stolen?

Trapped in Pharaoh's Tomb (#2)
The kids are trapped in an ancient Egyptian tomb. How will they escape before the air runs out? Will they be able to outsmart their rival?

Stalked in the Catacombs (#3)
Penny, Mark and David explore Paris . . . but their adversary is lurking in the shadows. Will they be able to outrun him through the dark catacombs beneath the city streets?

Surrounded by the Cross Fire (#4)
Rival drug smugglers will stop at nothing to get what they want. Why are KGB agents following Penny? Will the kids get caught in the middle of the danger?

Hot Pursuit on the High Seas (#5)
The trio is involved in an incredible hunt involving a catamaran, a Russian sub, helicopters, and more! Will they find the courage and creativity needed to escape from their predicament?

Hunted Along the Rhine (#6)
Tapped phone lines, hidden TV cameras, neo-Nazis, and a crossbow man make the kids' assignment for Mr. Daring's company not only difficult, but dangerous! Will they survive a bullets-flying speedboat chase?

Launched from the Castle (#7)
Exploring an old castle in Frankfurt, Germany, the kids witness a jewel heist! How will they foil the clever thieves' sinister plot after David disappears, Mark is captured and Penny runs for help alone?

Escape from Black Forest (#8)
Hunted in the woods like animals, the Daring kids rescue an injured German policeman and try to escape the attack of Iranian terrorists. Will they find their way in the unfamiliar forest?

Available at your favorite Christian bookstore.